Beyond Suspicion

Also by Tanguy Viel

The Absolute Perfection of Crime

Beyond Suspicion

A Novel

Tanguy Viel

Translated from the French
by Linda Coverdale

THE NEW PRESS

NEW YORK
LONDON

*This work, published as part of a program providing publication assistance,
received financial support from the French Ministry of Foreign Affairs,
the Cultural Services of the French Embassy in the United States, and FACE
(French American Cultural Exchange).*

*The New Press also gratefully acknowledges the Florence Gould Foundation
for supporting the publication of this book.*

© 2006 by Les Éditions de Minuit
English translation © 2008 by The New Press

Requests for permission to reproduce selections from this book
should be mailed to: Permissions Department, The New Press,
38 Greene Street, New York, NY 10013.

Originally published in France as *Insoupçonnable*
by Les Éditions de Minuit, 2006
Published in the United States by The New Press, New York, 2008
Distributed by W. W. Norton & Company, Inc., New York

LIBRARY OF CONGRESS CATALOGING-IN-PUBLICATION DATA
Viel, Tanguy.
[Insoupçonnable. English]
Beyond suspicion / Tanguy Viel ; translated from the French
by Linda Coverdale.
p.   cm.
ISBN 978-1-59558-156-3
I. Coverdale, Linda.   II. Title.
PQ2682.I316I6713 2008
843'.914—dc22

2007045954

The New Press was established in 1990 as a not-for-profit alternative
to the large, commercial publishing houses currently dominating the
book publishing industry. The New Press operates in the public
interest rather than for private gain, and is committed to publishing,
in innovative ways, works of educational, cultural, and community
value that are often deemed insufficiently profitable.

www.thenewpress.com

Composition by dix!

Printed in the United States of America

2   4   6   8   10   9   7   5   3   1

ONE HESITATES to do more than part the curtain and step aside, or perhaps strike a pensive single piano note repeatedly for overture, in the way of introducing a performance as delicate, complete, and fierce as Tanguy Viel's *Beyond Suspicion.* The book's reader will meet its opening pages with an intake of breath destined not to be completely released until its last lines have been reached. (You can certainly read it in one sitting, yet like certain novels of James M. Cain or Nathanael West or Paul Auster it demands recognition, in form and proportion, as a novel, rather than novella or story.)

The mode can be called classical, by now: Suspense, sub-class: Hitchcockian-Highsmithian. The lineaments of the tale echo a thousand others, creating a narrative spell trafficking less in surprises or shocks than in an undertow of doomy inevitability, inciting a reader's perverse craving to understand how the ancient fates will exactly be distributed among this latest cast of the damned. Noir is above all in the details, and Viel unfolds his with the restraint and confidence of a stage-magician mastering an auditorium with a mere deck of cards; but he does something more: by distilling his noir through an air of almost cosmic remorse, he dares to soft-boil the hardboiled, to tip it back in the direction of the romanticism the mode traditionally denies. The double benefit is to humanize his story while also etching it into a kind of mythic frieze: *'twas ever thus.* Much in the manner of Francois Truffaut adapting Cornell Woolrich in *Mississippi Mermaid,* or for that matter Camus adopting Cain's *The Postman Always Rings Twice* as a model for *The Stranger,* as well as Boileau and Narcejac deepening Hitchcock's own themes in offering his *Sueurs Froides: D'entre les Morts* as a source for *Vertigo,* this looks to be a particularly French response to noir: to purify it in the mode of a dream, to stalk its alienated essence. The most marvelous trick is that this pursuit, this distillation, uncovers noir's continuity with novels as apparently distant from this strain as Ford Madox Ford's *The Good Soldier,* or Henry

James' *The Wings of the Dove*—James's Morton Densher and Kate Croy, schemers destroyed at the crossroads of love and money, are not so far from James M. Cain after all. *Beyond Suspicion* is a tiny novel, but it is like an X-ray of an enormous one.

Jonathan Lethem
September 2008

ONE

THERE WAS THE WHITE CLOTH covering the table, a cloth it was now difficult to remember as white and gleaming in the sunshine a few hours earlier, set with crystal and silverware supported, surprisingly, by simple planks laid across simple trestles, which forced the guests to watch their feet all evening to keep from knocking the whole thing over.

How many were there, on that festive day, how many guests strolling through the garden with champagne offered in welcome by a row of waiters in short white jackets, so stiff and impassive you couldn't tell whether that stiffness and impassivity came from their bodies or those jackets, each waiter presenting his tray full of half-full glasses, unable to smile, trained to serve, and saying only a pleasantly crisp "Good Evening" whenever a hand reached out to claim a glass. "Good Evening," would come the reply, without their eyes meeting, guest and waiter both focused on the proffered glass, so proud, the guests, to be attending the wedding of Henri Delamare and Lise, a Delamare as well from now on.

All the same, it had been a lovely occasion, she like a teenager amid the invited throng, and the ostentatious splendor of that provincial bourgeoisie combining cousins, friends, and still those same stalwart waiters with their silver trays, waiters whose stiff bearing contrasted ever more sharply, as the evening wore on, with the increasing din of the celebration and everyone's champagned laughter.

And everyone had gone into raptures right away over the ocean view, chatting about the island glimpsed way out there, its contour, in this pellucid light, indenting the horizon and made fascinating by distance, but also through contrast, at the very spot where the sun would set a little later, darkening the water, the sky, the island of the same dull and somber shade, and where the moon, still later, would take its place within a millimeter to illuminate feebly not the island now or its rocky outline but that same weary table, tipsy with already vanished conversations, with the hubbub that would hover all evening over the festivities: jokes, laughter, pontifications, and Henri, that night, king of the world.

I'll just have to get used to this, I thought, used to this name and this house, to this unforgettable wedding, as Henri would say. Yes, it's true, I would remember: unforgettable. And how would I have managed to forget it, even ten years later, that moment when I'd found myself next to her, Lise, that same afternoon in the awful town hall to sign the registers, the mayor's big hand holding the book open at the correct page, his fat finger pointing out where to sign, and my trembling hand—what else could it do?—making all of it legal and proper, since I was the witness.

She was the one, Lise, who asked me to be the witness, and just the thought of backing out or offending her—I don't think it even occurred to me, not that or anything opposing the wishes of a sister, when I escorted her into the hall on my arm, with Henri behind us, and the only thing missing was the usual music.

But what was I doing there, Lise, in that official room that day, and later on the steps of the town hall, in that unbecoming suit, such a contrast with the brazenly virginal white dress of your marriage to him, what was I doing lining up now to congratulate you, waiting my turn with that same joyous expression swiped from all those other faces waiting to kiss you and murmur like everyone else a few well-prepared words in your ear: I wish you a long and happy life, I said to you, without a single quaver in my voice. But that handshake between you and me, Lise, you'd have thought it contained every secret in the world, ready to take flight over the town square, and nothing in the world would have induced you in turn to look up from the cold floor of the town hall, so appalling it was, that single glance you gave me and which hid so poorly the mingled feelings of shame and disaster inside us, shame and disaster, as if everything, everything that no one knew, everything that no one should ever know, had burst out in broad daylight, into the sunshine streaming through the windows, reaching everyone so that they'd turned to stare at me, all several hundred people who were about to kiss you and toss rice in your face.

A long and happy life, Lise.

The worst thing, the worst, is that at that instant I was truly able to think those words, with my hand clutching yours so tightly, the hand I would never have released had I not at that same instant caught the almost worried look of the man whose ring finger now wore a gleaming wedding band.

So proud as well of gathering together so many friends around this table, he would say—around the white cloth on which every knife blade still reflected the setting sun, the clearly marked horizon, and even the lush garden grass—when he could not resist rising to toast everyone, using that impossible expression perhaps only he still dared trot out: I should like to propose a toast. To Lise, of course, to this new sun in my life, he said, to all of you, he continued, to your heartwarming presence, and finally to happiness, he exclaimed amid the bursts of applause punctuating his words before he added, as the only somber note, silencing with a wave the clapping of his guests, his apologies for the absence of his brother, his dear Édouard, unable to be here this evening, he continued, but with us most assuredly in spirit.

He said one damned stupid thing after another that night, because of the alcohol and the attendant emotion, and because he was like that, Henri: When he drank he talked and spouted whatever came into his head. Several times that evening, taking me by the arm, he felt compelled to introduce me around: I'd like you to meet my brother-in-law, he said, puffing on his cigar, Lise's brother, Sam; his name's Sam, right, Sam? And I replied, Yes, quite right, Sam, and I smiled.

But above all, Henri went on, he's my new golf partner, right, Sam—isn't golf something?

That's one way to put it, I thought. And I turned around to pour myself another glass.

You know he's playing better and better?—launching himself for the fortieth time into the same golfing joke, his favorite joke whenever good manners and even snobbish condescension had long deserted him, the favorite joke he couldn't fail to trot out that evening on such an occasion. And for once there were people who hadn't heard it before.

It's the story of a guy who plays like a god, incredible strokes. He tees up at the first hole and swings: a perfect shot, a good two hundred and seventy yards, straight, just perfect. He walks up to his ball, gets ready to take another magnificent swing, but right before taking this magnificent swing, whoops, he gives the ball a little kick. So the guy with him says, Hey, watch out, that counts as a stroke. I know, I know, replies the first guy. Then he addresses the ball again, and again he hits a great shot, lands within three yards of the hole. Fine. Again he walks over to his ball, which is sitting pretty—all he has to do is sink a sweet putt—but no, instead he gives the ball another little kick. So the other guy sees this, goes over to him, and says, What're you doing—playing so great and then spoiling every shot with a stupid kick?! No, no, the first guy says, it's nothing. I'm just practicing for when I play with Sam.

And for the fortieth time it made everyone laugh, his joke, everyone but me. Me, I simply smiled because I saw Lise laughing merrily, and her laughter was hearty enough to cover my silence. But again that night he turned to me and added, We'll go out some Sunday, right, Sam?

And as usual I replied, Sure, Henri, sure.

But at every party there is a dead angle. At every party, I've told Lise, there are things one can do and that no one will ever know about. There he was, busy blustering about, having a thousand pointless conversations, so I picked my moment and took Lise's hand—or, rather, with a mere glance it was as if I'd taken her hand—and she joined me there on the dimly lit terrace by the house, and off we went into the darkness. She, drunk as well in the dark, staggering enough to tread on her gown, the music we were hearing fading further with every step cutting across the damp grass, me taking her arm to prevent her from falling. And it made us laugh, because of our already ingrained habit of scheming and dodging to meet for five minutes now and then, in no matter what barn or setting that would have us, so why not as well on your wedding day? I told her. She, glass in hand, on the verge of tripping, tried to avoid spilling wine on her dress. But I'm married, she kept saying, Sam, we mustn't, and she laughed even more the more secretive we became, intoxicated beyond all reason, she practically smirking, saying Sam, I'm your sister, let go of me, while she took my face in her hands, drawing it closer to her mouth, hugging me while pressing her lips to mine, making sure my mouth wasn't going anywhere soon.

But that just wasn't going to happen, in accordance with the infallible law regarding the combination of alcohol and desire capable of stifling any other so-called moral law, any other sense of decency at all, were it not for the ultimate threat, another man— who in this case was completely engaged for the moment in strutting around, that pathetic puppet husband who would still be making us both laugh for a long time to come, worse than a Charles Bovary, I thought, remembering that blank, self-satisfied gaze, that complacent impotence, and it was the same with him, not Charles but Henri, cast adrift with the first glances, naïve enough (or trying to be) to allow two people off in a garden on his wedding evening to frenetically undress each other, barely bothering to take advantage of the skimpy darkness and a skimpy bush to fall on top of each other, to kiss and laugh and even more.

But should one call that naïveté, when a widower of fifty marries a girl half his age and in what surroundings, so luxurious, almost indecent—words that had sprung often to my lips when I'd remembered how he'd met her, remembered everything that had led us there, to this absurd situation, I thought, absurd, I told Lise, from the moment when he had for the first time placed one hand on her thigh, holding in the other a glass of champagne that had cost him what it costs in those places: the price of luxury, I thought again, but this luxury included a soul, and this soul was named Lise, and Lise isn't just anybody, Lise is my sister, after all, I reminded her that evening, drunk as I was, and told her I'm going to go tell him, I'm going to go tell him that you're not my sister, I'm going to go tell him the truth, tell Henri, and tell him we had planned on a kidnapping, a kidnapping, yes, that's what my sister and I had envisioned, because it's a word that's easier to pronounce when one is plastered, *kidnapping*, I said again even louder. And she told me to be quiet now, to calm down, because it had become just a matter of weeks, a matter of patience from now on, and in any case, Sam, we can't backtrack now. And I kept babbling, laughing at the same time, at the very idea that you were my sister, Lise, it's absurd, I would have shouted again if she—placing one finger across her lips like the ultimate warning, caressing my cheek with the other hand—had not whispered: beyond suspicion, Sam. Beyond suspicion.

So I, lying there on the grass, lying snug against her, looked at the night up in the sky, the sudden darkness of Lise's eyes, and I thought about how we had wound up there.

TWO

BECAUSE THERE WERE ALL those evenings when, even sober, they managed to enjoy themselves—the company managers and men of the liberal professions, the car salesmen and smiling bankers—those evenings when the girls would turn toward them, and there was the pleasure the men took in making them almost into slaves, from the glasses of champagne offered the first evening in exchange for a hand on a thigh to those nights, never mentioned, that could drive their bodies to exhaustion and beyond.

The men felt at home there, although they dreaded being seen going inside, but when they shed their jackets in the cloakroom they shrugged off their cares, for drawn curtains safeguarded discretion and anonymity, so that from the street the place looked simply like a bar. As for being a bar, there was no mistake about that. An all-night bar, they call those places in a pretty paraphrase, to avoid any awkward words.

The girls had long since forgotten to complain or cry about them—those agreements made with this man or that, when, parting before dawn, they all knew what bound them together, what made them keep silent, and what they loved about the secrecy of it: that footing of equality the men felt with the girls and the girls with them. Equality in silence, that's what I've always thought about those evenings: that's what they shared, for real and forever, when for a few hours the insurmountable barrier would disappear between the worlds of these men, grown portly with age and excessively fine wine, and these smiling girls kept as if on leashes by their makeup and the intimate table lighting. There were elected city officials and the rich old men in their orbit, parvenus and local gangsters; they were all there, the usual suspects, as if corresponding to the archetypal image, perfectly established, of the world of dirty money and debauchery. And among the girls, all of them still forgetting that each smile required an effort, there was, of course, Lise.

I went to that bar a few times. With Lise it was different, I often thought, watching them at it in the back of the room, watching the men smile and clink glasses and slip their hands behind the backs of all the girls, with Lise it's different, Lise who for nothing in this world would have done more than be drunk at the end of the evening, Lise who'd learned all the lines that delay into impossibility the moment longed for by so many, who were ready to caress her shoulder or cheek with crisp new bills, with that way of saying all she had to do was stand up and follow them. But it was like a victory for them, that anticipation, that modesty in the face of temptation, she would say afterward, which rather made them feel she was giving herself to them even more, by putting them through extra paces to succeed. But they didn't succeed, ever. Not Henri, not anyone.

So every morning, like a dreary habit, she turned the key in the lock and that was like an alarm clock for me, toward five or six a.m. Her coat was hardly off before she emptied every pocket, which might hold fifty, sometimes a hundred euros she would place automatically on the table before collapsing onto the bed, with that impression she gave of going to bed each day just as things were really getting started, thanks to that absolute and inevitable time lag of the dawn that greeted her: tired, drunk in spite of herself, and slightly nauseated. And awake now, I would watch her, happening to glimpse my face in the single mirror of the single room that served as an apartment, thinking of the night she'd passed and the day dawning for me, less and less relaxed on the sofa, more and more with glass in hand and in the other, the TV remote, as if, by endlessly repeating the same useless gestures, I were temporarily erasing the image of myself on a sofa the whole goddamn day in front of the television watching everything: the news, TV movies, game shows, sports; but it's educational, I used to say to Lise when she got up in the afternoon, or else, it keeps me busy, depending on whether or not I felt strong enough to justify how I spent my time.

But she didn't notice anymore, what I did or did not do with my time, as she bustled about only to spend hers emptying the overflowing ashtray, stocking the fridge, sometimes turning off the television, and thinking out loud that all this was going to change, already proud of envisioning a tomorrow and dreaming, of course, dreaming of a better life, half convinced she was already living beyond the sea, beyond our drinks and the sad walls that battened down the apartment, and sitting balanced on a hundred thousand *maybes* she would replace indifferently with *soons* and *tomorrows*, when in a single evening she would be, in turn, a florist, politician, writer, the way she planned in turn to go back to school or become a pilot, and in turn would join me in a drink, then another, and I'll go to the States, she'd conclude with a smile. I would smile, too. Then she'd look up at the clock on the wall behind me and almost every time I could bet it was midnight, in that biologically regulated way I could have studied, parameter after parameter, the influence of everything on her words—the influence of nightfall, alcohol, the surrounding silence, the barking of dogs—and measured word for word the meaning of her pronouncements and the daily crescendo of her plans. Then, from one moment to the next, nothing more: silence, the ashtray heaped with butts, the slammed door, true night.

But if ever anyone rapes you, I thought each evening watching her go, he will die. And he no less than the others, I mean Henri, who'd been coming to the bar for months (since becoming a widower, he'd say, to clear his name) and always asked for Lise, or no longer asked for her, because Lise naturally—if he came in—slipped her hand under his elbow to welcome him at the door, accompanied him to his table, and sat down with him, next to him on the wide settee but really close, thigh to thigh in the clinking of their drinks. I saw them several times, and several times as well she told me about it: My best client, she still managed to say sarcastically, my best clients, she corrected right away, because inevitably, inevitably where Henri was, there was his brother, Édouard. There, I have since realized, were all the characters in this story. But that's precisely the problem—that your story, when it begins, has no idea who's coming along for the ride.

ÉDOUARD AND HENRI DELAMARE, ASSOCIATES: APPRAISERS/AUCTIONEERS said the business cards they had so often left with Lise, having already forgotten doing so, on reeling and tumultuous nights when the door closing behind them was enough to make them feel at home in the bar, in that freemasonry of desire, I often thought, in which one doesn't fear betrayal among brothers. And how many times, Lise and I, had we managed to laugh at them, at their impossible names, Édouard and Henri, imagining their mother and father bending over the saints' names in a dusty almanac, *very* dusty, we laughed, ruthlessly naming one Henri and the other Édouard. We imagined them as children, dressed in blue and white, coming out of every church in the *département,* destined for brilliant futures. But when you meet them later, those two, it's hard even to imagine them coming out of any church, just as it's hard even to imagine that they were once children, those two whose brilliant futures had arrived but seemed to leave their sparkle out in the street at night, willingly tarnished by the darkness of this underworld, the dregs of society, I'd say to Lise, and secret desires.

And not even secret, the desires they felt for Lise, especially Henri, his way of staring at her legs, of placing a sweaty hand on her knee or pretending to brush her breasts by accident but doing everything to make her give in, take the few steps that separated them from a room where all the girls fell on their knees before them, to make Lise yield in turn. She was unyielding, Lise.

So there is this curious and mathematical aspect of men's desire: that resistance does not beat down ambition but increases it instead, and what law of physics could explain this—what happened after meeting with rejection was that he wound up wanting more than her withheld body. He wound up loving her, that fool. Not foolish enough to say I love you, not foolish enough for a declaration like that, but foolish enough so that she came home one morning and told me: He wants to marry me.

• • •

I did hear that: He wants to marry me.

And how I burst out laughing at first, how I found that funny, wanting to marry Lise, to marry you, Lise; but do these people really think they can do just anything, don't they ever admit defeat? And she was laughing along with me, still stunned by such a proposition, stunned at having carried off what none of the girls had ever done, what was even tacitly off-limits on those nights, meaning the transformation into love of what at first was only longing for one body among many, for her body among many; and in the end it was bad luck, it was bad luck for him, Henri, to have ever run into her.

Marriage, I kept saying, marriage, as if in the worst of nocturnal worlds we'd found ourselves in a century gone by, and then him—he'd thought he was actually in such a time, a time of prudishness, of morality and propriety, in flagrant contrast with those premises where one buys even love, thanks to

Champagne and designer jackets, luxury cars and travel stories, when he'd talk for hours about going diving in the Red Sea, she'd tell me in turn the next day, where you see fish that aren't even in the dictionary.

Yet instead of laughing long and hard the way she should have over an idea like that, that such a guy would want to remake his life and would become so infatuated he'd want to marry her, instead of laughing, now she was like an astronomer who discovers a new planet, as if she'd found in such a proposition, encoded like a hieroglyph, an organized program for change.

I remember the sound of her voice that morning, both of us leaning on our elbows at the windowsill, both of us silent for long minutes, and everything that was now coalescing as if it were right there talking to us, with our eyes locked together, and I remember when she finally said, We can't pass up a chance like this, Sam.

But a chance for what, Lise? A chance for what?

THREE

So THAT WEDDING NIGHT we would have stayed there until dawn, lying on the grass with barely a breeze to waft away the alcohol, if a voice we were beginning to recognize hadn't interrupted us, a distant voice calling *Lise*, an almost anxious voice that made us realize it was now time to return to the party.

Now the moon was shining on the table, on the knives; and the glint of the blades had long since disappeared beneath the traces and smears of food and sauces; and the tablecloth had long since as well forgotten how to be white, supporting in its rumpled fatigue the almost-drained glasses tinted red with dried wine, a few lying on their sides like translucent artillery shells, except mine, standing up straight, refilled for the nth time. Perhaps it was three o'clock, four o'clock in the morning on the violet-stained grayish cloth and the few scattered cups left by guests after coffee or brandy, the aromas of which—mingling with those of the wine-spotted cloth, the cold cigarette butts crushed dead in the saucers, and the outgoing tide that also seemed to have abandoned the table—might well have nauseated the guests if they hadn't all, one after the other, already gone off to bed.

But not me. I didn't go to bed. Even though the party had lasted until four and felt as if it had been going on for centuries, I fell asleep right there, right on the table, facedown on a plate. There was Henri's voice still echoing over the dark water, his hackneyed jokes that had prodded laughter into exploding all evening long over the formerly white tablecloth, grown sticky with so much spit and vapid conversation, his voice I still heard like a ghost in my alcoholic slumber: So—we'll play a round of golf on Sunday?

Later on, that night would leave something like white noise in my head, neutral and subdued, which in its matter-of-fact evenness had gently rocked me like a chugging train. I was like a child, sleeping on that table, surrounded by no one, while all the others had gone to their bedrooms inside the vast house that would completely overshadow the garden in the morning light. That shadowy chill would awaken me, the chill of the damp morning and salt air, of the great house that overlooked the ocean and seemed never to have belonged to anyone else but Henri, who that evening had played his role as lord of the manor even more assiduously than usual, among the modern servants hired for an evening, dressed in a manner reminiscent, as Henri might have put it, of bygone splendor.

But the bygone splendor—that was long gone when I woke up that morning with a head full of regrets, simply because I'd drunk too much, too careless to drink enough water to stave off the wake-up migraine, the coated tongue, the legs twisted beneath the simple wooden planks laid across the simple trestles that hadn't toppled over.

Eyes puffy with fatigue, I would have paid a fortune to believe that the whole thing had happened only in a dream, paid a fortune for that split second sanctioned by my awakening, plumbing the division between sleep and reality, when everything is still confused. But after that, no: Lise came to her bedroom window and opened the curtains—I saw her. I even think she smiled at me; I assumed she'd smiled at me, because I couldn't see her well, with my eyes steeped in alcohol, and my inner drought, that same dryness the ocean breeze, fresh and humid, came to scoff at with its bracing vigor, its unconditional purity that had already dispelled the foul smell of the table, erased all lingering noise, and restored the garden to its silent virginity. On that particular morning I would have liked to wake up anywhere else at all— on a staircase, beside a highway, or inside a bustling refinery—and have been spared that confrontation with the world's natural ability to renew itself without me.

FOUR

When I rang the doorbell the following Sunday at Henri and Lise's there was the label on the mailbox with the two names elegantly penned as though on a calling card: LISE AND HENRI. There was the ringing of the bell you could hear from outside, and you heard that ringing go all through the house, then footsteps heading toward the door. It was Lise who opened it. But she wasn't Lise anymore to me that day; no, she was Madame Delamare.

It's an understatement to say that I'll remember that moment for a long time, hesitating between a kiss and a handshake, blushing and fumbling for words, before either of us had understood or processed who we were, standing there. You'd almost have thought she'd been living there all her life, she seemed so at home with the flowers and garden paths and everything. I left my golf bag in the front hall; she told me that Henri was running a little late but that he wouldn't be long, that I could sit down if I wanted.

For a little while that's how we were: Sitting in that armchair facing me, she didn't dare speak, and she fiddled with her hands, tugged at her skirt, looked at me when I wasn't looking at her and vice versa, and I didn't dare say anything either. We were like two crazy people keeping quiet and perfectly still, two neurotics intense and equal enough in their madness to briefly cancel each other out. Madame Delamare has large, limpid eyes; they seem even larger when everyone is simply waiting silently for the coffee to be ready and the husband to arrive.

The wedding, I ventured to say, though, was perhaps a bit much.

She did not reply, propped up like a dead animal cradled in the armchair, and it was almost disappointment I felt that day, projecting onto her clumsy hands the shame and embarrassment she'd felt in opening the door to me, serving me coffee, sitting in front of me, plus the niggling fear that Henri suspected something, that he'd guessed, not what was going to happen but that something was go-

ing to happen. It was the same thing, or enough—
something was enough to blow it. To blow it and do
it anyway, Lise often told me, because that's the risk
you take. The risk you take with everything in life.
That you'll blow it, but you do it anyway.

At times I managed to forget why I was there, facing her, yet not even considering the idea that our
hands might draw closer, and our eyes grow bolder—
no, without ever considering any of those possibili-
ties. Sisters are off-limits, said the look in her eye. It's
true: Sisters are off-limits.

As for that, I don't know what got into you, Lise,
what shot through your mind that day when you in-
troduced me to Henri, when instead of everything
that was planned and perfect she said: I'd like you to
meet my brother. She wasn't supposed to say that; she
was supposed to say *I'd like you to meet a friend of mine.*
What she said was *my brother,* and I heard her clearly,
as absurd, as insane as it was, I did hear "my brother"
and in my head I slowly worked out the equation:
there were so many things to think of all at once—
say hello without blinking, smile, find something to
say and at the same time think hard, figure out that if
I was her brother, then she, Lise, she was my sister.
And the only thing I managed to say to Henri in the

wake of all that was, Well, I don't need to introduce you to my sister.

But what came over you, I asked her later, to make you pass me off as your brother? And she just— she giggled, she said it was funnier that way, and I told her that I hadn't found it funny, that it had come *that close* to showing in my face, blowing the whole thing, and that, no, there wasn't anything funny about it.

And now you're not laughing so much, Lise, to see your brother with a golf bag in your husband's house; now you're not laughing so much in the silence of your new front hall, I thought as well, while the minutes piled up heavily on the table, on the cups she'd now set out in front of us to wait, like us, for the coffee to be ready.

Still, it's strange, I finally remarked to her, Édouard not coming to the wedding. . . . Don't you think it's strange? And she said, yes, she didn't know about that, but that I could ask him myself, since he'd be joining us at the golf club. I let it drop, simply saying, Ah, I didn't know Édouard would be playing with us, when I was already focused elsewhere, with the look of someone who'd come there to understand what he was doing there, in such a wealthy house, where the walls, the dishes and silverware, the fancy furniture dripped with so much money.

Because Henri was rich, with one of those fortunes that seem timeless, acquired ancestrally, then apparently passed on genetically to the latest heir, him, Henri, as he showed so proudly on the walls of the living room and staircase, the last of a lineage traced from portraits to photographs exhibited everywhere: the father, the grandfather, the great-grandfather, the great-uncle (a missionary), and the stern great-aunt, right back to the founding forefather reduced to the antique family formula of "the one who struck it rich," without anyone having cared for quite a while whether it was made on the backs of black slaves in the port of Nantes or laborers worked to death in some factory of the industrial revolution. Henri seemed merely to suggest, with that lofty look he favored, to imply that this fortune, this lifelong investment income, was something he had managed to increase, perhaps to double, thus escaping the threat hanging over every fortune, the implacable working of generations, he would be telling me often: The first one builds, the second conserves, and the third consumes. But for the moment, he would also say more than once, we needn't worry about that. And that falsely modest *for the moment* I could implicitly translate as *thanks to me.*

Thanks to him, I thought, thanks to him, and while considering the family photographs I couldn't help staring at the one displayed across from me, on the inevitable piano, next to the inevitable bouquet of roses that so beautifully matched the ivory-white frame imparting such a religious, and luminous, aura to the face in that same photograph, because I also knew that there, in that ivory frame, was the eternal memory of his first wife. Then—I don't know why—I picked up the frame and told myself that, yes, there were some points of resemblance between the two women, I thought, looking from the picture to Lise, from Lise to the picture, interrupted almost immediately by Lise's anxiety, perhaps her terror, Lise saying, Sam, don't touch that, and almost suggesting, I've since concluded, that with this single sacrilegious gesture I might have been able to bring a dead woman back to life.

Outside, the wheels of Henri's car crunched across the gravel; the hand brake creaked; the car door slammed.

But from now on Henri's wife is you, Lise, don't forget that, while through the slightly parted curtains

I could see Henri approaching the front door and preparing to open it, leaving enough time only to re-press the uneasiness in our eyes, to remake ourselves into brother and sister once more and then to tell ourselves, from the way he would shake my hand, the way he would embrace her, that, no, definitely, he doesn't suspect a thing.

So, Sam, ready?

Ready, Henri.

FIVE

IT'S A PENDULUM MOVEMENT to begin with, the arm moving slowly backward and rising in one sweep, the wrist cocking itself, bending beneath the weight of the club, like a trigger pulled back, a spring, ready to swing down again when the weight of the body moves from right to left; then the arms follow the movement, accelerating in the descent, carried along by the hips and the loins moving forward, and the arms hit the ball head-on in the sharp, snapping sound of the contact before continuing on their upward course, beyond the already initiated trajectory of the ball.

Like a priest tolling a church bell, the golfer executes his swing and follows with a nervous eye the distant flight and fall of his ball out there, two hundred yards away, where it continues rolling, rolling on toward the surrounding trees, trees that cover the course with their dense shadows, and it's because of these trees, thanks to some tiny slipup, that the ball often gets lost beneath the brown leaves of the chestnuts, there, at the first hole, in the tall underbrush that masses beneath the full-grown trees, so don't count on finding your ball: If it's in the forest, forget it.

But that's golf, Henri used to say, a long walk of frustration, he'd laugh. He often helped me and he was often the one who found my ball, because he played better than I did. That's normal, he said. I've been playing for ten years. But me, I knew; if I'd played for twenty years, nope: There are some people, that's how it is, they're better than others at certain things. And not even vice versa: There are some people who are better than others at things, period, I thought, watching Édouard play now, Édouard who had joined us there, at the first tee, and who played even better than his brother.

He concentrated, silently, taking one perfect swing after another, and the ball shot out each time for him to watch it land right where he had planned, after imagining the projected path of the ball; and it worked. The bag on its steel cart rolled across the mowed grass as I watched him walking quickly, already drawn to the lie of his ball and the next stroke. Then he turned back toward me, adopted a casual air, and with the distant expression of someone evoking imaginary quotation marks, Édouard said, *To see a world in a grain of sand / And a heaven in a wild flower, / Hold infinity in the palm of your hand / And eternity in an hour,* signing off with *William Blake* before setting out again.

With me it worked, that kind of phrase, as if he'd known his saying that would make my arm shake and throw off my swing so I'd play all the more poorly. *A world in a grain of sand*—I'd concentrate on that precise instant of the swing; *a world in a grain of sand*—I gripped my club and inevitably something would knot up in my stomach; *eternity in an hour,* I'd tell myself over and over, *eternity in an hour,* like a Hindu mantra that would have magically worked wonders. But the only magic was the ground slipping out from under my feet, the stiff wrists and taut nerves, and of course I shanked my shot; of course the ball veered off into the trees, five yards away, which made Henri laugh. But not Édouard; that didn't make Édouard laugh, for the very good reason that Édouard never laughed. In my heart of hearts I thought, watching him not laugh, just what is William Blake doing out on a golf course?

But the real question that, more than once I forgot to ask myself is, What was I doing there, Lise, on a golf course, wasting Sunday after Sunday getting trounced and talleying the strokes over par? Truly, I must have loved you, Lise, to want to *change my life* that much. So what I was doing there with them, albeit smiling and dressed like them? That's perhaps what is most incredible, on those days when we set out to-gether, the feeling of peace I felt then, telling myself that over and over—*change my life*—so I could bear it.

Everything's over par with golf, I've often thought: the Mercedes-crammed parking lot; the socks over the plus fours; even the hours spent in the club-house, the unspeakable clubhouse, drinking Irish beer and looking up at the TV screen, watching whichever sport was being televised on a special channel. Henri and I every Sunday at the bar, one eye on the screen, the other stingily employed in mutual congratulations on the day, the fresh air encountered under the trees, and shaking the odd hand of those also encountered every Sunday, the habitués whose scores for the day could be read in the way they puffed out their chests; and if you let them they'd give you a hole-by-hole account of their round, the drive at the fourteenth and the approach at the sixteenth.

How's your wife?

Oh, you know, Lise, Henri would answer, as long as she doesn't take up golf. . . . And that could have made them laugh for years to come, because it was golfing humor. So they laughed. Me, no, but they laughed. And at those moments I watched Édouard, because I was sure he wasn't laughing either, in that way he had of not listening to his brother's lousy jokes and of training his melancholy gaze upon the fairways stretching as far as the eye could see.

Ah, but you haven't met my brother-in-law, Henri would exclaim. He has just taken up golf—haven't you, Sam? His problem is fear, he'd continue. He's afraid of the ball. You have to face the ball proudly, Henri would tell me. If you're afraid, you're finished. Impossible to move properly, to swing correctly if fear is involved even slightly, even invisibly, in the performance of the arm. Fear in golf, he'd add, it's like the fear of death. And I looked at them, the guys still listening to him with the beer froth flecking their lips, giving them that bovine air, and in their eyes appraising me I saw written: He's some philosopher, that Henri. Letting me know like that how lucky I was to have such a brother-in-law.

I understand that you played with Édouard as well, one of them told me. A great player, a truly great golfer, he went on, turning toward Édouard himself. But Édouard himself had already, as always, slipped away without saying good-bye. I thought, an enigma, all in all, and one I'd have had to try deciphering through who knows what slogging, depending on the mood of the day, on his fresh or tired face, on the hour, on the sun dipping down or not behind the trees, on me examining him anew each time from every aspect only to fail to understand this: his absent smile. And Henri would endeavor to relaunch the conversation, because it's true, he said, it really is a stroke of luck for you, Sam, this opportunity to rub elbows with golfers like us.

I said that I was thrilled at the opportunity, yes— I said exactly that: I was thrilled. And I told myself, Well, that's that, I was talking like them. And I was still smiling at them. But I thought about those long hours of practice spent swinging a club, clumsily planting tees, and wrenching my back to swat a ball two hundred and fifty yards, days of effort thinking that a life can be redeemed by playing golf; and I thought how sometimes you can be falling apart without anything showing on the outside, nothing but the mediocre appearance of normality, without any signs of yourself showing anywhere.

That's where I was with my life, without anything showing, when Henri drove me back in the luxury car he said he hadn't paid a great deal for, because that's one of the perks of his profession, he said, to have an inside track on good deals, and one day I, too, would find myself getting some good deals.

True, it was magnificent, his car, and he always insisted on driving me, so I'd leave my poor excuse for a car in front of his house; that way we can go together, in my Jaguar, he insisted, which he remembered having bought for a song from an elderly gentleman no longer able to drive. He would basically have given it to me, he said, but I insisted on paying. On the whole, he's a vulture, I said to myself, who rubs his hands at each and every death, each and every wealthy widow who has a heart attack at the mere sight of him coming up the walk; and I imagined him in people's houses, drawing up an inventory of the Chinese vases and gold watches, the family paintings and Empire furniture, assessing each object at the price of his commission and calculating what he could spend it

on. But it isn't my fault, he said, if it's old folks who
are rich.

The car stereo was also a deluxe model, with remote controls he'd had installed on the steering
wheel. How many times during a short trip would
he fiddle with the volume of the various speakers
assaulting the interior of the vehicle, speakers ensconced in the front door panels, set into the rear
window shelf, and hurling at a hypothetical central
target—namely us, every Sunday, like clockwork—
the same exhausted Shostakovich waltz. It was like a
ritual, the Shostakovich waltz fortissimo, both going
and coming, with him so proud (the remote on the
steering wheel!) yet so uncertain about the usefulness
of a gadget like that, so for mile after mile he'd adjust
the volume non-stop, in the same way that if he'd had
solid gold windshield wipers, he'd have used them
in the middle of a desert. He was so busy fumbling
with the remote he hardly looked at the road, fine-
tuning the bass and treble, balancing the speakers,
with that Shostakovich waltz as the coup de grâce, I
always felt, and the worst part, the worst, I used to
tell Lise, is that he hums the damn tune on top of it.

I often said to myself, about these things, that
there had to be a last time for all of them, for setting

foot in his eternally luxurious car, listening to that eternally saccharine music to go play golf and shake certain hands, on those Sundays of sunshine and sweat spent trying to concentrate, because of the Shostakovich tune that evaporated too slowly in the pine-scented breeze and weighed on my movements like lead.

You'll get the hang of it, my dear brother-in-law, you'll get there, he'd say, poking fun.

But the only thing I'd be thinking at that moment, with my personal ineptitude and my personal secret, was: You'll fucking get yours, my dear brother-in-law.

SIX

ONE FOR THE ROAD, Sam?

On that particular evening, when we went into
his house for one last drink, when he'd shut the
heavy wooden door behind us, on that particular
evening it's certain that the sound of the latch had
already made him shiver, because of the silence in
the house, the night and the silence that for some
strange reason on that evening had oppressed him.
At times we seem to be driven by something stronger
than we are to do things that aren't like us at all:
This man who, from the very beginning of their marriage had let Lise go to bed alone, since he kept impossible hours that she had given up keeping from
the start, this man decided that evening, even before
pouring our drinks, to go up to her bedroom to kiss
her and watch her sleep, he would later say, some-

thing he would admit having never actually done before, preoccupied with his work, a man so busy, so businesslike—what thought, what feeling must have gone through him so that just then, on that evening more than any other when the latch clicked home, he felt like kissing his wife, Lise, and watching her sleep?

Several times as he went up the stairs, he would also tell me, he heard some unusual noises, as if they were too long to be simple creaking, too distinct to be the wind; but how would he, a man of reason and calculation, how could he have paid so much attention to some squeak that was just the shifting of wood, a whistling that was just the wind burrowing beneath the roofing slates until—it sometimes happened—they'd come crashing down? So when he reached her bedroom door and opened it, intending to go bend over her and kiss her in her sleep, he was already imagining her opening her eyes at the touch of his lips, with the door still quivering from his presence, the air in the room warmed by his body, but when he opened the door, instead of her sleeping in the moonlight, instead of her beneath the sheets, eyes closed and happy in her dreams, there was only the wind rattling the window and the curtain blowing inside the room, set fluttering as if by a devilish wind in the gleam of the streetlight outside, and her absence, the absence in the bed of her, Lise.

There was the darkness dispelled by the streetlight and the moon, the soft white radiance that filled the space, turning it more gray than black, and there was Henri, who had opened the door, planning to pull Lise from slumber, and now stood there before nothing but absence. It's as if one understands those things right away, the glaring truth when something is really happening, something serious and almost irrevocable, as if everything in him had known even before making sure, even before calling her everywhere or wondering if she'd gone out on her own or fallen asleep in some other room in the huge house; but in truth, no, it was as if it had been written in the story he'd been telling himself since coming home, in the hallway followed to reach this bedroom, and he had come on purpose because he knew, something inside him knew that she had vanished.

What he did first was rush instinctively to the window and peer out at the garden lying below in the luminous night, looking everywhere in case something or someone . . . but he found not a wisp of reassurance. Although he did feel something, he would later confess, simply because the thought had occurred to him, because he'd picked up on a hint of suspicion floating in the somber atmosphere of the place: He'd had the feeling he deserved it.

He went out into the garden, into the indifferent coolness of the night, and he called her, called behind every tree and bush, without a reply. He went through every room in the house, all the lights on everywhere, running, panicking, calling. But Lise didn't answer, not once, because Lise wasn't there anymore, neither there nor close by, he understood, when he sat down on her bed, when he put his hand on her pillow where the soft hollow left by her head was still visible, and when he stayed there a moment, waiting for *what* from the waning night and the diabolical wind? Nothing, nothing but stunned astonishment, his temporary ally. At that very instant, looking everywhere for traces of her, he noticed a letter sitting there, a few words left in lieu of a woman's head, a woman's body, hers, Lise's, replaced by these few words written in black in a confident hand: *If you want to see her again, wait quietly tomorrow by the telephone.*

I did not go upstairs with him, even when he screamed *Lise* all through the house, I didn't go up; I stayed there, at the bottom of the stairs, one hand on the knob at the bottom of the banister, looking upward and asking, What's going on, Henri? Tell me what's going on! But with nothing showing, oh, no, nothing showing.

I can see us both in the living room, our still-empty glasses in front of us, awaiting developments. He handed the short note to me, and I in turn was rather stunned, it was so well done. But what to do or what to say I had no idea, just that I be there, and that we both be there, him sitting with his head in his hands, smoking cigarette after cigarette, constantly smoking. How many hundreds of times would he read that single sentence before understanding it, before each and every word agreed to make sense in his head?

We didn't talk much, except to wonder what they might do to her or not, comforting ourselves with the idea that they were interested only in his money, his fortune that he was ready to hand over a hundred-fold; at that moment he was of course ready to do it to see Lise again. Then everything will be fine, I said—if you cooperate, everything will be fine. And I kept insisting, as if to reassure myself and him at the same time, that a kidnapper or a gangster isn't a butcher or a killer, he just lives off the contract he offers you, and if you honor this contract, so to speak,

I told him, what I mean is, if you accept the price he sets, then you can do business with him.

But why me, he was sobbing, why me?

Because you're rich, Henri, because you're rich, while a glance around that living room rapidly tallied up a certain number of paintings, bibelots, and mirrors that littered the house, and because he could sell them rather quickly at any routine auction for tens of thousands. Maybe you'll have to sell some things, I said.

He was now clutching his head in his hands, looking even more distraught, the forehead tight against his palms, frozen in that pose of tearing out his hair, practically a statue because of his hands, motionless, gripping his hair all ruffled by his clenched fingers.

I won't sell a thing.

What?

I won't sell a thing.

It was like a reflex in his mouth, to say no that day in that predicament. For a moment fear, dignity, and the disappearance of Lise all bowed before a reflex: I can't.

And he added, breaking into the silence that followed: because of Édouard.

Because of Édouard? I simply repeated like a surprised echo; but Édouard, I thought, Édouard has nothing to do with this.

He won't like it, he continued. If we have to sell, if we have to pay, he won't like it.

So perhaps something showed in my face at that moment, like a twitch or some tightness in my cheek. But no one's asking him to like it, I said—it's *your* wife who's been kidnapped from *your* house and it's *your* money they'll be asking for.

That's just it, he replied, precisely. It's a very complicated business. All that money, this house.

And it was as if the trees themselves were about to speak, to untie the knot of this tale that seemed inescapable from that point on and which already figured in his calculations, a new setup, with him looking at me, silent, as if he'd waited for perfect quiet in the humid air of the living room to tell me.

All this isn't completely mine, Sam. That is, it's all legally mine but legally means nothing, nothing at all, he said, weighing the silence in the hollow of the sentences and half sentences he was intoning mechanically in that lull of waiting, that state of fatigue, suddenly almost smiling to be unburdening himself of a weight he seemed to carry there, in the secret of that house and himself, to be telling that

Tanguy Viel

old, old story, he said; it feels like only yesterday, he said, that day he was remembering now, that particular day, the truth of which he seemed to owe me, apparently eager to shed light on something that had happened twenty-five years ago, he sighed, twenty-five years.

But instead of actually talking, instead of expiating I didn't know what disastrous mistake, he prolonged his sigh with a single fixed and significant look, a single look directing my gaze to that photograph on the piano, you remember, still that same photograph of that same first wife, a photo now gaining in depth, in relief, suddenly taking on a third dimension, this photograph that now seemed to hold within its white rectangle all the rest of the story. But what, Henri, what do you mean?

She should never have been my wife, Sam. She should have been Édouard's wife. She and Édouard, Sam. She and Édouard, he repeated, getting back to his feet to move closer to me, in the armchair where he went to sit down before lighting an umpteenth cigarette, thereby leading me to understand that, yes, that woman—Édouard's former future wife—by some strange twist of fate had become his. Then without my offering even a single word or question, he merely concluded: That's how it is, that's all, it happened like that, and now she's dead and now I live here and now this house and the money up on the walls—today all that belongs to me, but it also belongs to Édouard.

SEVEN

I DIDN'T UNDERSTAND EVERYTHING, Lise. But I thought of you, I thought about everything we didn't know in this business, about this shady clan we'd waltzed into, this fusty money, this so-often-absent brother. For the first time I thought, like you, that now it was too late, that we couldn't back out anymore. So I picked up the anonymous note still sitting on the table and I read it out loud: *If you want to see her again, wait quietly tomorrow by the telephone.*

Wait quietly, it says, wait quietly, I repeated to him; that means we shouldn't tell anyone, because you shouldn't try outsmarting people like that—you follow me? First off, if they're doing what they're doing, it's because they're professionals, so, no, don't call Édouard, because Édouard might blow the whole thing, I said.

He'll find out—he'll definitely find out. You don't know Édouard, he said.

Actually I do, I replied. But I didn't say anything more, I just kept insisting that we shouldn't ruin everything, and that Édouard—well, he wasn't my brother, of course, and he was a very fine person, of course, but Édouard was not involved in this affair, I said pointedly.

I went on, homing in on everything that was still free in him so he would understand, understand that it was between him and himself, meaning him and Lise, because what you don't realize, Henri, it's that people who do this—you can't imagine the entire nights they spend organizing every detail, and the determination that drives them right up to the end. Unlike you, they know everything that can happen and the decisions to be made, everything, from beginning to end. What they say is: If he comes alone we make the exchange, but if he pulls a fast one, we kill her or we split in the car hidden in the barn—in any case we take the girl with us, unless he comes alone and goes along with the switch. And in that case, Henri, your wife will be home tomorrow evening.

From habit or perhaps impulse he took a golf club that was lying around and began to play with it like a

kid who doesn't know where to look or what to do
with his hands, and that way he managed to lie to
himself for moments here and there and think it was
all just a huge joke, all just a fake, he finally said. But
it was for real, when the sun floated some dawn over
the garden, and Henri went back up to her bedroom
as if to verify in the clear light of day that it truly had
happened, dazed as he was even more by the passing
empty hours and no sleep besides. So when he came
downstairs again, he'd come to his senses.

I'll pay, Sam, he said, I'll pay. You're right, I
shouldn't tell Édouard—he won't know anything
about it. After all, he said, it's true, it's a kind of business deal, he said.

Now that, that irritated me a bit: a business deal
about Lise, dickering over Lise. That's my sister
you're talking about, I almost said. But I didn't say
anything. Or rather, yes, I said: Of course, Henri, of
course you'll pay. I'll help if I have to. My sister, my
dear sister.

The hand hanging onto the banister, the clammi-
ness of the hand and the heart surely pounding—it
was a kind of corpse who was looking at me, one
who no longer knew what was making him suffer or
on the contrary exciting him, between his heart beat-

ing ever faster and the growing desire, the irresistible desire to kiss her, he told me: I just wanted to give her a kiss.

Now he was looking at me as if my presence were bringing him bad luck, or as if I were the one he would have liked to sell for a ransom the amount of which he didn't yet know but was only already speculating about, as if he'd thought himself back behind his lectern driving up the bidding: a hundred thousand, two hundred thousand, five hundred thousand.

I know what I'm talking about. I've seen them in action, too, auctioneers; they'd sell their mothers as easily as armchairs, I told Lise every time I didn't go along to the auction house, and we would wind up, she and I, behind the iron shutters we closed in the afternoon to make ourselves believe it was night and which, simply by creaking, awakened our desire and drove us into each other's arms. It was like a reflex, the front door hardly shut when she came upstairs to my place, the slatted shutters filtering the daylight and the density of the sky, and then we were like dogs alert to the signals, with that heightened way we had of making love sprawled out on the bed, already anticipating the awkward arm reaching for the ashtray by the lamp and the taste of the postcoital cigarette, thanks to spending whole weeks like that, enclosed by those pale brown walls, beneath that light so unworthy of us in that too-short time we were allotted every week, those hours stolen to make those moves we had for each other, when we still managed to meet, taking advantage of his time at work, an auction or a meeting at the office, and we imagined him taking inventory of the dead houses, the dusty furniture priced according to the mood of the day, both of us lying on the bed thinking that at that moment he was rattling off figures in the auction room, three thousand on my right, four thousand on my left, and the falling hammer we imitated with a *Going, going, gone!* before cracking up with laughter.

But I wanted that to stop quickly, those hours owed to love, there on the wrought-iron balcony waiting for an ending, something that would terminate the strain of this secret, the Tuesdays and Fridays, the *maybes* and the *won't come agains*, the minutes counted, the partings in the street without good-bye kisses; it had to end quickly, I told Lise, because the passing time was wearing us down, and we'd need to be patient for several months in order to feel we were out of danger—yes, we had to go beyond the point of no return so we wouldn't see (on our lips, in our eyes) our minds flooding with anxiety, and all the fear it cost us to endure what was still trying, in our laughter, to become obvious, inevitable. A kidnapping, Lise: Do you know what that means?

And now—I knew what that meant, looking at the pale and nauseated face of Henri Delamare. So then how much for the ransom, Mr. Auctioneer: five hundred thousand, a million, two million? I thought about that, when I left him the next morning at around ten o'clock because I had things to do, so many things to do, with a bottle of Champagne on the passenger seat, and Lou Reed singing on the car radio. I thought about Henri's own car and about how we would never have listened to Lou Reed in his car (Henri so alone in that empty house now suddenly so big, waiting for the phone call that wasn't coming and thinking over what I'd said, that she would be there this evening) and about how it really hurt me to imagine her, Lise, sleeping soundly again in that bedroom.

Then the phone rang at about eleven o'clock and in an almost calm voice Henri said Hello.

Listen carefully to me, Henri: if you want to see your wife again, we advise you to cooperate. Listen carefully again: at eight o'clock tonight, you will get into your car, alone, with a million euros; you heard me, Henri, a million euros. You will drive north for exactly six miles; there is a forest along the shore, and at the first intersection you will turn left, and you will drive through the forest to the dunes. Park there. You will see an abandoned chapel on the dunes. We'll take care of everything from there. Come alone, Henri. Don't try to outsmart us.

EIGHT

Now all we had to do was wait; meanwhile I laid my head on her stomach and was looking at the very yellow sun high in the very blue sky. I remember—since at that instant I was tempted to kiss her and simply told myself that it was not the moment—the bottle of Champagne stuck there in the sand, distorting the horizon. What with all I had drunk, and not having slept, there were moments when I managed to forget what we'd decided on. Even Henri, at that point—I would have liked him to be happy with us. But that, Lise told me, that is not possible. As if sometimes you had to remind yourself what you're made for and the pacts you've made with yourself. In practice, though, the question disappears—of knowing or not if one is made for something: you act, that's all. So, Lise, for the time being you were

still my sister, and we'd see it through to the end, because we were in too deep, much too deep.

Soon we change our life, she was saying, her head
resting on the sand, and she was holding straight out
in front of her that dollar bill he'd brought her back
from the United States. Not from the United States,
from the States, she preferred to say, pronouncing it
so weirdly, with that accent imitated from an American actress, as if in saying it she'd felt herself possessed by a promised land constantly postponed into
the future—New York or why not Chicago, as long
as her imagination had long ago transformed it into
the vague, far-off place of the perfect life, life
changed into solid gold.

Life changed into dollars, she corrected, but
knowing full well that there was only one person who
could bring her dollars like that, one man alone much
richer than she and I put together, and that this man
was of course her husband. So, because he was rich—
and that's part of why we were there, lying on the
sand with the tide coming in, the smoke from our
cigarettes drifting up from our lips to evaporate
above our faces, above the shadow cast half by the
panama hat tilted over my forehead, half by our really
black sunglasses, each pair reflecting, as in a mirror,

the other's absent gaze. So this bill floating in the future and the blue of the sky confirmed what she was dying to say and had been saying for so long, that we had to change our life, she insisted.

Once someone told me, she said, there was a dollar bill and on it he'd drawn a heart or something like that and of course he'd spent it in a store. But ten years later, he's way off in another country, they bring him his change at a gas station, and bingo: halfway around the world he winds up with his bill from ten years before with the drawing. It's incredible, no?

When you get right down to it, I said, money's a bit like a boomerang.

And she kept contemplating George Washington's head she was holding at arm's length so that you couldn't tell who was staring down whom, Lise lounging on the sand or the tranquil countenance of the American president, like a *Mona Lisa* from the great beyond silk-screened in millions of examples and who there, in that single one brought back for Lise, still seemed to have a soul.

This bill, she said, is like the hunter's decoy: All you need is one to bring in the others.

So then I looked into the reflection of her glasses, and I could see, in front of the sun shining through this smoothed-out bill, the face of the American president floating on a blue sea, foaming and darkened by the slick blackness of her glasses, as if front and center in its very own stage setting: the dune rising at the back, the rocks we'd clambered over to get all the way down to the warm sand swirled up by the wind, the distant clouds still hesitating to close up the sky. There's always a bit of a breeze at this spot on the coast, more rocks than sand and the sea can kick up quickly, but we'd thought it over carefully, and it was perfect here, perfect for the exchange.

A simple exchange, Lise was saying, because it isn't a kidnapping, if we love each other it isn't a kidnapping, or else it's a fake kidnapping. We were laughing but with the revolver close by, because even for a fake you have to take precautions, because, I told Lise, this kidnapping is fake for us, not for your husband, not for the police, only for you and me, and with money things are never fake.

My boat was not far away, sheltered by the rocks. Just in case, we'd said, we had to get away fast. I was thinking of: everything we're going to do with that money, with you, Lise, when we'll be rich in a few hours—a million euros, that's something, Lise, a million euros. She corrected me: Let's call it a million dollars, just for fun. And in her voice I heard the words as if italicized: *a million dollars.* That's how it is; with Lise there are some words that are like alarm buoys, invisible sirens, with that intonation she knew how to use on certain words when her normal voice conveyed nothing special, so, as she lay there on the beach in the sun that seemed to dissolve her words even as they left her lips, this million dollars echoed all the more inside us as if onstage in a theater. I thought, it's like air flowing all around and in the middle there is this marmoreal dream—all those bills already packed into the black suitcase on its way here, and me already dreaming we'd then be on our way without him.

He had to arrive, Henri, at eight on the dot. He had to come. You had to come alone, Henri, come alone, I begged, when we'd walked up from the beach to the appointed spot up there on the dune, that small chapel weathered by the salt air on the edge of the pine forest forming a sort of dark backdrop for the scene playing out: the two of us impatiently watching the gulls screech at one another on the dune, waiting in the shadow of the cold stones, near that door sagging for a hundred years now, since no fisherman's wife ever comes here anymore to pray for a husband's return. Me, though, I did: I prayed for a husband's return.

I no longer know today which it was—the sun glinting off the windshield or the engine sound, so recognizable, of the 1956 Jaguar—that signaled his approach, but I saw him, coming from the main road through the trees toward the chapel, toward the two of us, my weapon already aimed at him, and my fear, the fear that he had not come alone and willing to play along, Henri, with the car door now slammed and locked, and Henri instinctively following the lead of the small suitcase in his right hand.

I held the revolver in one hand, Lise's hand in the other; she was completely hidden while we waited for him to reach the chapel door and set down the valise; and better for him that he doesn't flinch, or else, or else. . . . And he didn't flinch, as if he'd drawn sudden confidence from the simple fact of the money he'd be leaving at the foot of this church, at this altar, I'd think for a long time afterward, like an offering made to the gods, in dearly bought forgiveness. During those long seconds bringing him closer to the enemy, but closer to his wife as well—his dear wife over whom I'd seen him shed so many tears—during those long seconds I had time to wonder if it was really necessary for him to walk along that sea, so familiar and so restless as well that evening, as if the sea itself were trying to speak and add a touch more ceremony to this unlikely rendezvous, I was now thinking with every yard he covered across the short grass of the dune in the fading backlight from the setting sun, as if out for a simple daily walk, a simple daily walk, I kept telling myself, only this time there was anxiety there, too, about that dreaded moment when he would set down the suitcase and then leave, not turning back but retracing his steps, in silence, when yet again each second would carry its weight in waiting, in the light growing ever paler as he'd move off without unclenching his teeth, waiting for the door to open and her to emerge, Lise, for her to emerge at last so that he could dry his tears.

But they weren't tears streaking his face in the eight o'clock sunlight still dazzling him a little, not tears anymore but great drops of sweat on his cheeks. An animal, I thought him at that moment, carrying that valise, its lock glinting, to pay—to pay, I thought again, everything you can. With each step he took on the damp green ground I saw him packing the bundles one by one into the valise, pay, I went on, keep paying, and each step seemed worth five thousand dollars.

Everything was working, everything was going to work out; the light was streaking and glimmering through the forest, that green and black strength of the trees in serried ranks forming behind him the scenery of his slow progress, slowed by wariness but almost, it seemed, by the calm of someone advancing without second thoughts, impelled by the necessity of what was coming, to pay what she was worth, Lise, because you were certainly worth that, Lise, much more than that.

Perhaps through pity, certainly through haste, even before he'd set down his valise, even before he'd come quite close, I asked Lise to go outside, as if to prove our good faith, without making any sudden movements; and she went out, Lise, very quietly. He stopped for an instant, then continued his slow advance, as if in symmetry with the one Lise had begun, same speed, same rhythm, as if both of them had feared some false move on my part, so that the ground beneath their feet seemed no longer like thick dune grass misted by the sea but like explosives, dynamite, or eggs they were trying not to break, and this made her—especially her, Lise—seem ethereal, weightless, almost like a ballerina in the way she took each step, almost as if she also wanted to tell me that she was in no hurry to rejoin her husband.

But you don't need to worry about that, I murmured; we'll soon be far away together, Lise, far from a guy capable of buying his wife back, a guy capable of believing that a few bundles of money would buy her back, her, showered with Champagne and fancy clothes, Lise, so perfect in the slanting light bathing the suitcase bulging with her price. I saw, Lise, I saw your face on five dollar bills, like a real *Mona Lisa* this time, your face and flowing hair reproduced two hundred thousand times. And I saw him now appearing to meet you and the hand he would have liked to wrap even harder around the handle of that valise guiding him all by itself, the valise that seemed to know the way by heart, and it all seemed to stretch out for miles. Keep walking, I kept saying in my unfathomable inner chaos, churned up from who knows where—the sky, the very waves witnessing this countdown under way and echoing with the gray keenness of the waves the violence of everything welling up in me, in her, then crashing along into him, him again, his gaze slowly dulled with panic seeing her come even closer just when I was about to shout: *Put it down, go on, put down that valise,* and he was going to bend over, only a few yards away from me— he still hadn't seen me—he was going to set the valise down on the ground, certainly very carefully. He was going to do it.

So what happened then, I don't know—a branch, perhaps, a stone on the ground or sheer nerves: he stumbled, Henri.

NINE

I SAW HIS BODY as it fell at a slant; I saw the valise released, as if flying, tumbling through the salt air, falling so slowly to that ground way too hard for it, saw how it exploded from the force of the fall, how it landed and burst wide open.

It burst wide open and I saw the bills take off like ordinary paper. That's what I saw most of all: ordinary paper. Not real money with real denominations but blank paper, perfectly blank paper that flew through the balmy air, not bills, just ordinary white paper, virgin, immaculate, cut out the way children cut out coloring paper, and it had jumped out of that valise and was now escaping from it whirling like bogus manna from heaven, taunting us in close-up, clinging to the rugged stones of the chapel and flaunting its laughing virginity the way a gull would have landed there on the worn edges of the granite, that blank paper that was like a full slap in the face.

I burst out laughing; I laughed in front of Lise who was screaming, screaming as never before, Lise, who had also seen the blank paper swirling among the trees, the paltry price he was ready to pay to recover her, not one dollar, I told her, just look at that, look at what you're worth, not one dollar. I laughed even more savagely as she ran suddenly toward me in fear and the uncertainty of which way to turn. And me: But what am I going to do with you now? Just that: What am I going to do with you now, *not one dollar?*—beside myself with rage or disgust, my first impulse to slap her, because of her worthlessness in her own husband's eyes (not one dollar—has that sunk in?) now that I too couldn't see anything more than those bills stripped of all value, nothing more than the dead loss of each one of them. So what do we do with all this, Lise, with this million dollars, hmm? With this *fucking million dollars?*

At that moment, I heard his voice, Henri's, all surprised and befuddled, Henri still sitting on the ground from his fall, as if asking a question of the sun: Sam? Sam, is that you?

It was as though that sobered me up in a second,

hearing my name there, out loud, in the open, but what's possessing him, Lise, what's possessing him to call out to me? And I felt the stupid impulse to say no, that it wasn't me, that it was a mistake, my body now paralyzed as if by a mind cramp, a heaving up from the depths bringing everything to the surface now, those moments I recalled when he would place his hand on her thigh, and his question kept coming at me like something slashing my skin: Sam, Sam, is that you?

You could have shouted the names of the trees, Henri, the names of the sun and the sky, of the night and the topmost branches of the pines; you could have named the whole world and the creatures inhabiting it but not me, Henri, not me, while he kept making it worse, repeating more confidently now, Sam, Sam, not realizing that his every mention of my name was like a bullet in his brain.

Yes, Henri, it's me, it's been me for a long time now, of course. Beyond suspicion, I repeated with a finger across my lips, because you were far, weren't you, from knowing or supposing that lurking behind every scene, every move, and every night, there I was, off in a corner leaving you a free hand, Henri Bovary Delamare, because everything since your marriage has been a minefield, Henri, and you never knew a thing about *our* story.

No, you didn't know anything about that, you bastard, but now you do, and how many bullets I fired before hitting him, his body falling heavily face forward onto the cold dune while he began to moan with pain from the metal inside him, Bastard, I repeated more quietly, calmed by the single bullet that had managed to strike him in the right thigh, and astonishing myself at having succeeded in hitting him at ten yards, in inverse ratio to my nervous state, my compulsion, Lise said, because you're a compulsive, she would later tell me so reproachfully, because it's true—we hadn't planned on the sound of a shot.

If I could have, that's for certain, at that single moment I would have given his wife back to her husband, my Lise to her husband, I thought without even noticing the absurdity of the phrase so appropriate to the absurdity of the situation, because it was absurd, him already on the ground, bewildered by the rush of blood, the wind whistling around, and his body would have liked to crawl to his car even at the cost of one, two, three shots right in the heart, when he abruptly realized what had happened there, the entire future laid out in that single gunshot, in his physical collapse happening there and becoming, warping, into the collapse of a life.

So, Henri, what do we do? What do we do now? That's what I read in his haggard face, almost stupefied with fatigue; I saw the lack of understanding in his eyes, in his bloodshot eyes. And I reflected that I must look the same, with inflamed eyes and jaundiced skin, both our faces drained by the ordeal, bereft of thought, but where physical traces of ourselves survived, for instead of our brains it was more like our nerves thinking for us.

He was there, almost unconscious, and Lise was no longer screaming but picked up the echo: And what do we do now, what do we do with him?

Let me think, Lise, give me a second to think. But can you call that thinking when the mind takes off with the speed of a bullet?

He has to keep quiet, I said, keep quiet forever. No one knows anything except us, no one knows anything about you and me, or the money—that's our chance, Lise. He drowned, I said, he came to go swimming and he drowned.

You drowned, Henri. What do you think of that?

No, he said, no, there's no need, I won't say anything, I swear I won't say a thing.

And I said something equally absurd: Okay, Lise, here it is: We'll report him missing. And rather quickly I thought of the cold and amnesiac sea because it alone knows how to keep quiet, Lise; we have to take him far away to be sure that even the sea won't have a sudden burst of recollection, to make sure that it forgets even his name, Henri Delamare. And he begged us and moaned so much that I might almost have given in to his pleas and let him go again if Lise, more lucid than I was, hadn't looked at me clearly, so clearly.

It didn't take us long to figure out what we had to do. Undress him first and leave his clothing on the beach so that a fisherman or anyone else up early the next morning would find them and worry that an imprudent swimmer. . . . There you are, it's so simple, I said to Lise; we just need to get rid of the trousers. Because of the blood, I said.

And now we have to move him, we'll take him to the boat. We'll use his car, I said, to get him to the boat, find the keys in his pocket, Lise. And I drove his car, his Jaguar, across the dune to where he was. We lifted him up as best we could, this stripped body, still bleeding and growing heavier with his exhaustion and his tears, because he was weeping, Henri, weeping heavily, and we placed him in the trunk. He fit snugly inside, in that peaceful fetal position, like a child dropping off to sleep, with only the bloodstain to reveal that his sleep would soon be deeper than that of a child.

I started the car up on the dune and drove a short way down to where my boat was. I can tell you, even for a distance of five hundred yards, it's something to drive a Jaguar with an auctioneer in the trunk.

But how quickly the sea changes in that part of the world, turning suddenly so gray, and we had to embark on that nasty mirror image of the sky. Sheltered by the rock, with the old Zodiac straining to break free, we got the body out of the trunk and into the boat, Lise and I, Lise still rattled by what we'd just been through. Henri's body wrapped itself for a moment over the rounded edge before tipping inside onto the wet wooden slats, awaiting nothing more but me, while I was undoing the knot proudly made that very morning with an ease that had seemed like an omen of good fortune. But fortune, I thought at that moment or perhaps later, fortune was not the right word, that day.

What would have been the right word beneath that sky so gray—with that anthracite column of clouds at the horizon, like a pillar of wind and water gradually overshadowing the sea, turning it gray as well—and then Lise turned her eyes where she hadn't looked before, where something in her had resisted or forgotten to look, out to sea, toward the ocean exposed to her gaze along the entire length of the horizon, and she understood, screamed and understood at the same time: Sam, there's too much wind, you can see there's too much wind!

So what, I said, it's a squall, just a squall, I explained to Lise, fate's parting shot at us, the sky's last dirty trick to try separating us, but me, I know the sky's going to lose. And to my mind, more than to hers at that instant, it was obvious that leaving everything as it was would be like putting one's hands up in surrender, so I don't call it an alternative, Lise, more like a clear duty, an order vouchsafed by some *Deus absconditus* saying to go out there—into the open ocean, the wind, the elements—and finish this business once and for all.

Don't you come, Lise; wait for me here if you want, I told her, and let me handle this, while she sobbed over the hours that had passed and bargained with herself to stave off a nervous breakdown. I kissed her; she wrapped her arms around my neck and kissed me too; and she took my panama hat. I'm keeping it, she said, as a hostage. And she almost smiled.

But I wonder even now what we were doing out on the sea that day, Henri and I, all darting or brilliant sunshine gone, only dense clouds shedding their overflow of water, while the wind had strengthened beneath them, with only we two left on the rolling sea, we two and that old lawn mower motor that seemed to struggle alone now against every foam-swollen wave that lifted it out of the water, leaving the propeller to race in the empty air before getting a grip once more beneath the surface and driving us forward, as we bounded rather than slipped across the heavy seas, pockmarked everywhere by that fine rain wetting down both air and waves, as if pricking the sea with hundreds of thin needles, vexing it, the sea heaving up, almost rearing, as if in response to the prolonged irritation of the insistent droplets, now that I think back on it, like sewing machine needles at top speed that left a lunar landscape beneath the on-coming fog—or at least something like how we imagine it, the moon, meaning, at that particular moment, someplace surely more peaceful and a lot drier. I believe I would have given all the ransoms in the world to have been there, on the moon, and to feel six times less the weight of his body drawn down to the deep.

Now you're going to have to go, I told him, as if I'd been speaking to a man with all his wits about him, and he, lying there like a fish flopping about in the hold of a trawler, still found the strength to cry and beg for pity. But the fear of death, Henri, it's like fear in golf: You have to face death proudly, Henri. But this very word *pride*—which he had known how to use and derive like a mathematical term, as if the idea of pride itself flitted permanently overhead, a shadow cast, skittish, always available enough for him to appropriate it at any moment, at any aristocratic moment, he said, of that false aristocracy that conceives of itself, decodes itself, even defines itself according to that principle, of class, mastery, decision—that very word *pride,* as I was saying, seemed to have deserted his emotions, to have gone quiet or to ground in some corner of himself where none of his nerves had the strength left to ferret it out in the damning silence of the waning day, because he'd have swiftly understood that it was all over, hardly time enough left for a last sob, and perhaps to try believing that he'd be found still alive. Yet, in these dark places, you know you will die long before you do. I imagined him, powerless to abridge the agony, those long hours in the chilly sea surrounded by true night, in water that was suddenly noisier than he had ever noticed before and allowing him only the right to reflect upon his fate, and enough time to shiver, thinking of his wife, and decide that, yes, the world at that point was only this: the cold and the night.

I imagined this for him and I believe it was pity that gave me the courage to put another bullet in him, his terrified face begging don't, but I swear, I truly wanted to spare you the worst, Henri, to spare you the unbearable. Afterward, there was the lost sound of a body in the water, the sea foam barely visible in the somber twilight, then I went back to where I'd tied up the boat. Lise was waiting, wearing my hat, and she'd done everything necessary: waited for me without crying. We were tired.

But there was always another chore to take care of, something else not to forget, a fatal detail. I tried to take stock of the situation in my head, wondering, is there anything I've overlooked? I went over all the details as if I were crossing items off a grocery list.

Get rid of the body: done.

Clothing on the beach: done.

Cleanup of the car: done.

Collection of the blank pieces of paper: done.

So was it also like grocery shopping when, even with a list and the best will in the world, you go home and there's still something stubbornly missing?

TEN

OUR BENUMBED BODIES.

My trembling.

Lise's face.

Obviously we headed for the first bar we could find, so long as it sold beer, I thought, plenty of beer to put things somewhat back in perspective. I don't know if we talked at all before sitting down, before scraping back the chairs and placing our order, before lighting cigarettes almost at the same time. We wouldn't have said anything in any case except empty phrases, words to paper over our real predicament, because anything else you might have said, Lise, so many images of what we'd do together with that money—love in four-star hotels and silk bathrobes, posters of Acapulco and sports cars, the bright future you predicted for so long—it all seemed now like just a mirage, a magic potion of phrases that sometimes managed to become pictures, dimensions, colors, but which from then on would remain a dead weight in our mouths.

It's just that through impatience and as a way to buck ourselves up for the job, we'd put everything we had into it, into this dream of money, by fair means or foul, fair or foul, I'd said so many times until the image of that million dollars became as swollen as a balloon about to burst, a real bomb that had then simply exploded without us knowing for a long time now whether the idea or the thing was more tangible. I believe the money had been in our dreams for so long that we'd finally put it under a bell jar.

I remembered that empty suitcase, that case full of not a single dollar, and I wondered how it was possible, looking at her, not to let go of at least that: some money. I looked at her again, and in my head this scene played out: imagining her body on the auction block, the inventory of each part of her—a foot, the back of her neck—and I imagined how many millions I'd be willing to bid. Then I felt ashamed of my thought. I've often been ashamed of everything in my head.

But what the fuck are we doing here? I wondered

several times, she and I casual as could be, as if we had nothing special to do there or anywhere, when me, I was nothing more than a body bone-tired of staring at the now rainy night, our shadows under the lights pooling as the silent minutes went by and time ran away from us like wind across our skin. We hardly dared look at each other, in hopes that the whole thing—that infernal night and the passing hours— was just a bad dream and that soon, soon we'd wake up at dawn.

It's an accident, just an accident, we each repeated, as if we'd expected someone, somewhere in the street or at a neighboring table, to overhear us, because we'd been trying so hard to figure out how all that hadn't happened, Lise, how nothing else had ever begun except our own story.

Now, Lise said, we're like clandestines, illegal aliens. Her saying that—to my mind it was as if she'd given up on that other expression she had used so often, that we would change our life, which she no longer said with that smile now forever lost, replaced by this deathly pale and stony face, when maybe we should still have had the courage to smile and do that, change our life, like a slogan stolen from poetry, or advertising, or politics, I no longer remembered, so strong was my momentary impression that this phrase was like an injunction delivered from far away, from an inner world that was like a revolving beacon that regularly trained its harsh light on me, on the image of me.

In *clandestine*, I said, there's *destiny*.

We stayed like that a long time, whole seconds, not saying anything else, either of us, except what lingered on perhaps from that word *destiny*, what had clearly surfaced from that remark, the two of us still silent with those endless cigarettes, knowing that we were now entering a time of tension and turmoil that would easily rival the storm outside and the spindrift on the windows, in this gloomy bar where her hand on the table automatically wiped away the ashes scattered in front of her, whatever anxiety or relief she felt at imagining what would come next betrayed by her way of collecting the ashes, then sweeping them away so quickly to the far end of her silence. Then, I don't know why, as if I just couldn't resist, I had to add:

It was your idea, Lise.

But it was as if I'd been talking to a wall, her eyes lower than the ground itself, Lise stubbing the cigarette out in the ashtray in front of her, standing up as she did so, as if she had leaned on that same cigarette to support what was left of her body, and as if anger, shame, or resignation were driving her to leave so abruptly. She moved so fast I had only time to hear her footsteps on the tile floor, see the bar's front door open, then slam shut, and her boots made no sound in the rain, while I noticed the waiter looking up to heaven and then, wiping off my table, as if it were some humdrum proverb, he said, Ah, women.

ELEVEN

WHEN YOU LOOK at the sea on the day of a spring tide, you wait for the next wave, for it to be higher, to make you forget the one before; you wait and look and this goes on and on because the idea never stops, of watching one melt away and another well up. That's how it is; you'd stay for hours until the wind dies down or the swell subsides with the outgoing tide.

But it wasn't a day for contemplation, that Monday, with the search on in all directions, the helicopter crisscrossing the sky, the coast guard, the gendarmes with their white motorboats, and the dogs on the dune sniffing around as if working an avalanche. Instead of contemplation there was more like the fear that a wave might heave in more than sea foam—the body of someone who would make the front page of the local newspaper the next day. An auctioneer drowns: an entire paragraph on the danger of spring tides and another one on the clothes found on the beach, because it didn't come back, Henri's body, of course not—the sea is much too vast, indifferent to the affairs of men, the article had said in conclusion. So a rough sea and a few items of clothing carelessly folded in the hollow of a rock: what would lead anyone to imagine that on this very spot someone was killed because of a little pride?

A little money, I also thought, lazy enough not to want to untangle what parts in this business had been played by money, by pride, or else simply by love for a girl not made for all this. And I thought as well that at times what's called madness is precisely that confusion, from a few electric words that go insane inside you.

And yet it's curious how sometimes you can be calm because everything is in an uproar, calm because you simply don't know why you would be—on the verge of tears and hysterics, on the verge of running off across the dune without ever looking back, but no—you're just calm and you put a good face on things, the face you'd had to scrub free of much more than the salt or the smears of dirt clinging to the cheeks, when you had to look mournful this morning, with that sadness borrowed from the faces of others, without anyone, either the cops or the gawkers, being able to distinguish between playacting and the grim mask of true sorrow.

Her sorrow as well, Lise again, disheveled on the beach and sleepless but who'd had the strength that night to pick up the phone and with an anxious air that wasn't faked and a voice to match had called the police to indicate her distress over this absence, my darling husband, she was saying again this morning to the police chief, and crying.

I would have liked them to wrap this up quickly, this useless, really useless search, I felt like telling them, because the sea is too deep for the helicopters and the dogs, and by this time the crabs on the bottom are better bloodhounds. There was Lise still at my side, like a sister beside her brother, and I thought that this was logical, that for the moment I had to remember this, that I was only that, her brother, while at that same moment, pretending abruptly to seek comfort in my arms, clinging to me as if she could hardly stand, at precisely that same moment she whispered in my ear.

There he is, look: Édouard. And Édouard was indeed approaching us, looming ever larger as I caught sight of him, with his confident bearing, his measured tread, his black suit, and my conviction that he was bringing with him more than mourning. There was a pause; a firm handshake, a nod. I didn't wonder how he'd happened to land there that day, at that time; I didn't have the time to wonder about all that, because in my mind it was faster than that, because he had to be there.

You had to be there, Édouard, inevitably. But I didn't say that aloud, I merely experienced those words inside me like a mental invasion, those words and in front of me his face that had taken possession of every thought, every idea I had, so that all I could stammer out to him was that I was terribly sorry about his brother.

It's a dreadful thing, I said.

Yes, a dreadful thing, he replied.

And he was already turning away from me, from Lise whom he had only briefly hugged, as though it were his duty to scan the horizon in hopes of bringing Henri back, and also as though, at that moment, he had wanted to say that we did not belong to his world.

It's unbelievable how much he looks like his brother, I thought again, while they all continued searching, with their awful dogs I could already imagine fetching Henri's shredded body in their mouths, barking, wagging their tails at their handlers. The searchers were looking everywhere, in the little chapel and the forest behind it, their eyes inspecting the ground and the foot of each tree; and I wasn't calm anymore, not calm at all, after begging the salt air to erase the evidence, after seeing Édouard cup his hands to his mouth and shout his brother's name with renewed energy.

But they didn't find any evidence, nothing that led anywhere in the end. Hours later we all found ourselves back on the dune, around the car sitting there as if nothing had happened, the Jaguar shining in the sunshine like a pet waiting for its master's return. You'd have thought we were at a car show, from the way that car could make people forget that a man had disappeared, with everyone, cops and onlookers, casually standing around, checking out the perfectly polished chromework, the gleaming radiator grille, the beige leather upholstery, and the six long letters stretched across the trunk hood: JAGUAR.

It's definitely clean, I told myself, at the same instant hearing the keys jingling nervously in his hand, Édouard's hand, as he spoke to Lise.

I'll stop by Henri's house this evening.

He didn't say *your house*, Lise; he said: *Henri's house.*

And with that he slipped behind the wheel of the Jag, leaving Lise and me to watch him drive away.

We watched him quite a while, staring at the steadily receding rear fender, relaxing, thinking: things are improving. Those cars, I said, you've got to admit they're something, aren't they, Lise? But Lise wasn't listening to me, still staring at the car in the distance, and I asked her if she was all right. But she still didn't hear me, didn't turn her head—Lise, what is it, something wrong?

Your panama, Sam, what did you do with your panama?

I could still hear the sound of Édouard starting up the car, Édouard who'd gone from zero to sixty miles an hour in twenty seconds and whom we were now watching vanish down the road, but I know that in my own head I went from zero to sixty faster than that when Lise brought up the hat, and faster than the twelve lined-up cylinders of his engine rumbling in the distance, the battery of neurons in my skull flashed like lightning.

I ran a hand over my head, as if to repeat the question in a gesture. But I don't know, Lise, what did I do with my panama, what did I do with it, help me out here, Lise—my heart racing with so many bad questions, reviewing the whole nightmare of the previous evening, But I gave it to you, Lise, when I went out in the boat, you said for a joke you were keeping it as a hostage.

Then she brought a hand up to her mouth like a child realizing it's done something bad, and she reached out to point toward the exhaust fumes supposedly off in the distance.

The trunk, Sam, it's in the trunk, in Henri's car.

Édouard's car, Lise. Édouard's car.

TWELVE

THERE WAS SILENCE that afternoon in the dead man's house, and that was normal because Lise was a widow, and that, I reminded myself, I must not forget. Édouard served the drinks, as if he were in his own home, and because he said so, too, that the place was in a way his home. Lise said nothing. And I even less. It was like a wake with the body missing.

All dressed in black, Édouard: he seemed to be in mourning like an Italian woman, although given the granite terrain and the lush dunes, more like a Breton peasant, except that his thick eyebrows and impressive height made him nothing like a woman, oh no, nothing like a woman, Édouard, whose presence seemed to control even the pattern of our glances. Whenever I was about to put my glass down on the table, his eye would follow me, that suspicious eye I'd noticed right away and which seemed constantly to question my presence, asking, Just what are you doing here—what are you doing in my brother's house?

But I'm *her* brother, I tried to remind myself again, and as her brother I see my sister whenever I want. I knew, though, that I wouldn't have been able to say that to Édouard, or to endure his eyes on me from now on without wondering if or suspecting that he'd understood everything, that through some impossible fluke he had already known everything for a long time.

Whenever I was about to put my glass down on the table I remembered the car trunk, imagined Édouard opening it, and just the thought of him with that panama in his hands made me bring that glass back up to my lips and take another swallow. I'd have kept on drinking a lot longer if Édouard, instead of allowing me the time I needed to regain my composure, hadn't broken the troubled silence of our three tormented souls and finally said, settled like a prince in the best armchair: I don't believe it was an accident.

There was that window behind him, darkening his form. There was that statement like a detonation in my skull. To keep my glass from trembling or tipping over, I held on to it tightly as I set it down gently, as gently as possible.

Really? I said. I seemed like someone asking an impersonal question, as if Édouard had been talking about the stock market or the weather, as if he'd said I don't think the hydrangeas will last long this year; and the two of us had been having a quiet conversation about this and that, while he, as if to heighten the effect of his words, had stood up and walked quietly toward the window.

Now he was looking out at the orchard, the dozens of apple trees bowed down with the weight of their fruit, fifty apple trees perfectly aligned and perfectly spaced, which the wind had so often bent and twisted like old men, most of the trees as old as the same half century flowing in his veins; and Édouard now suddenly became a shivering ghost glued to the windowpanes filled with black sky, the sky coming through the denuded crowns of the apple trees to smash into those panes between the chipped white strips of the window frame.

No, he said again, Henri would never have gone swimming at that spot.

I looked down, my only reaction, while inside me

something was already thinking that it was a lost cause, only a matter of hours. Just call the police, I thought, and get it over with. I had time to imagine my hat taking flight over the dune, whirling around like a dead leaf before returning on its own to glide into the trunk of a Jaguar. I saw my panama entering the gates of a prison, in the hands of the cop at the entrance who played with it in front of me, removing his cap to set my hat on his head, and I saw the navy blue uniform and the white panama, the wisps of broken straw over his pathetic mustache and his pathetic smile saying, Doesn't take much to amuse us, does it?

But Édouard, still leaning against the wood of the window frame, did not say something like I'm going to inform the police or There will be an inquiry. Instead of that he turned toward Lise and said, Now all this is yours.

He swept his open hand around in a half circle, as if he'd been gathering everything into his palm. It was as if he'd laughed to see her at the head of such a phony fortune, as if he'd already programmed its imminent collapse; he even seemed to be saying or suggesting with an insinuating tone that it would all crumble, all fall at his command, leaving nothing between him and her, her and me, me and him—nothing but that statement delivered like a judgment: now all this is yours.

But what was that to Lise at that instant, to me, what was that, the fortune of a dead man? Cardboard millionaires, I thought, as though we knew in some secret cranny of ourselves what we really were.

No one said anything more. Each minute took forever. We were waiting for him to leave, for him to stand up and then go, since that had to happen at some point, that he'd be good enough to cross the threshold in the other direction. Get out, I prayed, get out, and I felt as if I wanted to drive the devil from the house. He finally stood up. But he glanced at the golf bag in the front hall, as if struck by an idea.

Tomorrow, Sam, I'm planning a get-together at the club, he said, as a tribute to Henri.

I lowered my eyes again to indicate reverent contemplation, de rigueur whenever Henri's name was mentioned.

It would be nice if you could be there. I believe that would have pleased him.

Of course, Édouard, of course.

Well, then, until tomorrow, Sam?

Until tomorrow.

And the door slammed shut.

It would surely have been better if we'd told him everything, Lise, if on that whole evening behind the closed shutters only the chandelier had seemed to hold still in our minds and all the rest had been only a slow-motion whirlwind of sentences petering out, of botched stories cobbled together from the infinite run of images, thoughts, digressions that would have made a coherent narrative. Everything would have started to go around and around, Lise, revolving endlessly on that interminable evening—the furniture I would no longer have seen save through a veil of tears, on my knees before him saying that we were completely pathetic, yes, pathetic; and that nothing had gone according to plan, absolutely nothing, because we hadn't understood a thing, because we were pathetic, I would have repeated before the billowing cloud of his incessant cigarettes, so that this whole business (which he would have considered from afar, from on high, from that leather club chair in which he would naturally have ensconced himself) might be placed firmly in his grasp, so that he might crush us with it, that story of ours. It would have been better, Lise.

But that's not what we did. That's not what I did

when we were both left there to go around in circles and turn everything over in our minds, trying to figure out how we could have wound up like that, with that unlikely sequence of events crowned by that stupid detail, I told Lise, that stupid hat he would brandish like a trophy before every police force in the world. I paced up and down, erratically, in every direction, like a madman, almost staggering around the furniture and just trying to figure out what I was doing there that evening in Lise's house, and waiting for what?

There's no reason, I said to Lise, no reason to open that trunk. Or else. . . .

Or else he knows, said Lise.

I reviewed everything he might or might not know about it all, including the dawning idea that Henri, as a last resort, Henri, alone and feverish with waiting, Henri had told his brother about it in the end; but that wasn't possible, I thought, that's not possible, because then Henri wouldn't have come with the fake money, obviously not—if he did that it was precisely so as not to have to talk to Édouard; because if he had talked to Édouard, then he wouldn't have come alone, or else he wouldn't have come at all, or else he would have informed the police, or else. . . .

Or else Henri did tell him, yes, but Édouard let him go to the rendezvous. He knew: I was mulling this over as a thought darker than the rest, and of course it commandeered enough space to over-shadow any alternative, any peaceful vision or even one open to other futures besides the one with my own body in a cell nine feet square, and above all, Lise's body in a nine-foot cell, and the thick sound-proof wall that would separate us; and I was already imagining Édouard with my panama on his head, be-cause suddenly it occurred to me that he'd seen every-thing, Édouard, that from the shelter of the trees he had watched the fake money fly into the air, he'd watched his brother die, and suddenly I thought—he's the one who packed the valise.

But if he knew, Lise, if he knew, then by this point he would already have told the police, by this point we'd already be dealing with the steel handcuffs and flashing blue lights. He doesn't know. He knows nothing. So we mustn't do anything rash, we mustn't panic; and you see, Lise, the panama, I might very well have forgotten it in the car some other time, and that hat might very well not even be mine—he has no proof, you understand, no proof against us.

And now it was my turn to pick up the golf club

that was still lying around there, and I gave it a practice swing. I almost felt like getting out a ball and taking a shot at it, across the living room.

But what are we going to do, Sam? What do you want to do?

Nothing, Lise. Nothing. I'll go play golf tomorrow, that's all.

And I was struck with that inevitability, already envisioning nothing else but the green realm of a golf course, and thinking that basically I was made for this: playing golf.

THIRTEEN

THE GREEN LAY BEFORE ME in a gentle concave slope and my ball had to start descending slightly to the left of the hole, taking advantage of the slope, to wind up on the right. It's always harder to putt downhill than up, Édouard said. A good golfer always manages to tackle the cup from below, avoiding the downhill approach whenever possible, because of this rule: you have less control over a ball rolling down than one rolling up. So he considered my position, he looked at the ball and the distance to the hole and said, Right, go for it, Sam. You have to get this one in. I think there was a slight pause, but what I'm sure of is that he added: Imagine that you're playing for a million dollars.

I looked at him, trying to read behind his furrowed brow to see if he was serious, because those words had given me a kind of jolt—a million dollars, words the color of the sky that seemed to have changed so quickly, and I thought: He can't be saying that by chance, he can't be talking about a million dollars by chance, no, not a chance.

I remembered William Blake, I recalled the grain of sand and that whole world therein. If William Blake had been in my present situation, he certainly wouldn't have written what he did, but I thought he might have come up with something like *A million dollars, and the whole world comes tumbling down.*

Édouard was looking down at the ground. He was gently swinging his club the way a pendulum would mark off the seconds left in a life, and I watched him without knowing what to do. Well, play, he said, play. So I pretended everything was fine, I took my putter almost calmly, I bent over the ball almost calmly, I prepared to forget everything, to look only at the grass, the white ball, and the cup eighteen inches away, and I took my stance. I looked at Édouard again, waited for him to say something once and for all, I looked back at the ball, and shot the putt. And made it.

The thing is, I said for a laugh, the only difference between gold and golf is a single letter.

But when I looked up again to force myself to smile and pretend everything was fine, at that moment I now know that I was not dreaming when I saw him there, before me, wearing my panama.

Not a laughing matter.

He kept gently swinging his club and looking at the ground, like someone about to say something momentous. But he didn't say a thing, Édouard; he started walking to the next hole—or rather, yes, he said very softly, he said, Might have a bit of rain before this evening.

It was then, perhaps, that I had the impression certain things were beginning to make sense, that all those months spent trying to concentrate calmly on golf courses had been scripted for this day, this particular moment. I was not afraid; it was like a communion with nature all around me. How many times had I heard that, how many times had I laughed to hear them, all those stupid golfers, communing with nature? But that day, with Édouard standing before me, in silhouette, with the tall trees and the water that was already reflecting sunlight onto him—with all that, yes, I finally understood the communion, when all is silence all around. So, play, he said. And I would have liked to reply, No, why bother; it would be better if we had it out with each other or dealt with it right there, with that seven iron he kept gently swinging in front of him, eyes downcast, tense, unreadable, riveted on the ground because of that business about the money, because of that million dollars and that panama masking his eyes in shadow.

I thought about the number of times I'd lost the ball in the water at this second hole, thanks to the hundred and thirty yards you had to clear to have a chance at reaching the other side. This time, though, the water, its depth, the silence nesting in the surrounding pines—this time I didn't thank heaven for having come up with such trees, dense and evergreen, allowing only enough light to filter through so that people could be seen but became invisible when illuminated from behind. I swung, I hit the ball like never before, and I cleared the water. I should always play like that, I thought, with a seven iron hanging over my head.

Now I was expecting him to club me in the temple, the forehead, the back of my skull, and in a way that was a relief, because it was like a weight that would have rolled away along the grass.

Just what is it you want, I said, what do you want?

So he in turn stepped up to his ball, and in an al-most natural tone of voice he said, I want Lise.

The air was split by his swing, by the sharp snap of the shot, by the ball whistling straight on its way. But up there, up there in the gray sky, when the ball in its curve was lost for an instant against the light and the water was hushed beneath the whip crack of its launching, there was Lise's name flying high with the ball. It wasn't anything like a face or a name, Lise, or a brightness or a memory, but only, at that precise in-stant, the immobile implosion of everything, as if my brain had collapsed further inside me, perhaps like what happens at the core of a black hole. I thought: That's it, Lise, a black hole.

I'd rather be in prison for life, I said.

He didn't reply. He didn't reply because he hadn't listened, because he was watching his ball land and stop over there, right in front of mine, beyond the water, on the velvety grass of the green. At this mo-ment his ball and mine, I thought, have more to say to each other that we do. But I remember with what condescension he added, his face radiating triumph and mastery, Tomorrow at four o'clock, the auction house: my silence for Lise.

FOURTEEN

THE PORT WAS RUSTING AWAY. The warehouses were rusting. The sheet iron was rusting. The boats were rusting. The sea was rusting. Even the men, the few strays who continued to stir up the dust on the docks—no one knew anymore if it was the sun, the salt, the iodine, or just the reflection of the rust everywhere that had reddened their skin. The roofs were rusting, the breeze blocks were rusting, the trucks, the rails half buried in the ground and half covered with dry earth, the tanks in the distance that had once stored oil—everything was rusting. The horizon was rusting. The cranes rose from their rusting platforms; the cargoes sat on their rusting blocks; the factory chimneys stood out, rusting, against the sky. I've taken stock of these past few days. All those years watching television, haggling over programs with a sigh, all that went by in a flash when compared to these, the last few days.

Aside from that, nothing. Nothing but the self-same feelings. Same fear. Same rust on my iron balcony. The tide high at first, then low, then high. The rocks covered with water, then uncovered, then recovered with water.

I remember your face that morning, Lise, the two of us leaning on the railing, the port in the distance preventing the city from drowning. And I kept staring and staring at your face. But it was as if I were seeing a ghost in spite of the glow of your skin, and your red skirt, and your smile so fresh—something like a specter, because your eyes, your eyes above all, seemed no longer to belong to you.

I remember the two of us silent for long minutes, and I remember everything out there that seemed to be discussing things with us as we stared into the distance, and your silence, your lengthy silence that still drums at my temples.

I'll do it, she said. I'll go see Édouard.

You won't do it, Lise. I'll go to prison if I have to but not Édouard, I said, not him.

Then I'll go to prison with you, she said.

She was putting her hair back up, holding it in

both hands, a hairpin in the corner of her mouth, as if she'd said something normal as the day was breaking, when you could just barely distinguish the distant division between sky and sea, way out by the last ships on the open ocean. Leaning with all my weight on the iron railing of the balcony, I thought it was working loose because I couldn't feel a thing in my legs anymore, or in any other part of my body, nothing to guarantee that gravity was still in force, that the laws of physics still governed a normal world. I tried to picture that, Lise in prison, not Lise in a nine-foot cell, not Lise locked up and crying, but maybe the day after, fifteen years later: Lise stepping back out into the street, the rendezvous we would have made, her dull, lifeless hair. I tried to picture that. Fifteen years later. But I couldn't. I saw Lise and the absence of Lise.

You won't go to prison, Lise.

Then you won't either, Sam.

I tried again to look far away, as far away as possible, but I didn't see them anymore; at that moment I didn't see them anymore—not the roofs, not the boats out on the ocean, not the horizon, just nothing more than tattered scraps of color or fog that mingled with her voice, which was vaguely threatening—

but to tell me what, now, that I might understand? Nothing, nothing except her voice itself, able to sound without a word or phrase managing to cling to the tone of that voice, nothing else but the slippage of syllables slowly absorbed in transit from her to me to become phantoms, vapors gliding into the blur of myself and my vacant eyes, there where my mind held nothing more than this idiotic question, this idiotic question about whether on any one day two people on this earth have ever seen the same horizon line.

She began to cry. But I wasn't looking at her anymore, or listening to her, so that once again her sobbing was lost in the air without me knowing what it was in the sound of her voice that had set everything wavering unstoppably—her face that I no longer imagined except as veiled by our now mutual tears, among which appeared insistently these last words she added: It was my idea, Sam.

FIFTEEN

It was your idea, Lise.

But I'm the one who told you to wait there, in the car, saying I wouldn't be gone long. I'm the one who went inside, into the main room of the auction house, my form reduced by the walls of mirrors that enlarged the space and in which, a few times, I avoided my own eyes. I would not have been able to say at the time whether my uneasiness or shame was seeping out of my skull into the air-conditioned hall, but I felt the drops of sweat on my forehead betray the layer of foundation applied to my fever-flushed skin in an effort to look like a normal client. At the reception desk, I asked if I might see Édouard Delamare, Maître Édouard Delamare, I added.

I was told that would not be possible because at that moment there was an auction going on in the main room. Of course, I went into the room, dumb enough at the time not to have understood what was really going on—an auction, at *that* particular hour, on *that* particular day?—dumb enough to go inside casually and look for him behind his lectern and find him, of course. But at the same moment that I saw him, I also saw behind him, in front of me, for everyone to see, my panama hat.

Obviously.

Obviously, I told myself, while I slipped into the crowd at the back of the room, alone in my head and feeling the presence of those curious onlookers standing behind me, like fifty spotlights tracking me, the sweat already trickling down my back.

I still remember the amount in play when I came in—twenty-three hundred euros for I don't know what knickknack—and my heart was already pounding to hear that: twenty-three hundred on my right, twenty-four hundred in front, Édouard conducting from behind his lectern, and one or another of the buyers preparing to raise a hand for twenty-five, and twenty-five again, sold, with their own way of bidding, all with the same self-satisfied, almost impassive air, who simply by batting an eye could increase their bids with the auctioneer. I remember that fat man in the third row who kept bidding on anything and that woman behind him who raised her bid without making a sound, and Édouard in a dark suit, his voice always steady, like a machine to make you break into a sweat.

Because for me, there in that provincial auction house, it was as if priceless paintings were being sold, with van Gogh's *Sunflowers* as the highlight of the afternoon. Whereas that highlight was actually a small straw hat Maître Édouard Delamare had just summarily presented as soon as he'd seen me walk in, a panama of Ecuadorean straw.

This magnificent panama, Édouard said specifically when he placed it on his desk, showing it to the audience, turning it so that everyone could see it was in perfect condition. And for the first time I saw Édouard smile. Nastily, but he smiled.

For this handcrafted straw hat, reserve price one hundred euros. And I knew there, in that hell, that it was my turn. I thought of you, Lise, waiting for me in the car. I thought how good it was that you wouldn't see this. Édouard looked over at me, as if to explain to me that the moment had come, the smile still on his face and the fever invisible on mine. One hundred twenty, I heard, one thirty. My hand declined to be raised, as if it had told me that it knew what it had to do, that it would decide, not me; one forty on my right, one fifty on my left, and still I kept quiet, one sixty, said Édouard, one sixty once, one hundred sixty twice, while he had closed down his smile from that moment on to send a silent order that meant: Now, Sam, now. So without anyone seeing either my fear or my doubts, considering my move, simply raising my hand no higher than my head, and without a tremor in my voice, strong enough for all to hear, I spoke up: Two hundred.

Two hundred.

You have to have attended an auction once to understand that first bid, the first time you announce your presence, at that instant when for the first time you're the one running the game and abruptly become the center of attention. No one turns around, no one looks at you, but you, on your own, you look enough at yourself to know you're at the very center. It's like a breath that drifts all afternoon across all those faces, a soul that turns and stops at each person who makes a bid. Then at that moment, when you know you have to get going, that it's now or never, your head spins, wavering with hesitation, and your hands shake, because you can never know if it's the right moment, if the auctioneer will understand and if you're credible in an auction hall. The auctioneer's gaze is like the breath of God alighting on you and filling you up with numbers, at the simple wave of an index finger, passing over all others, brushing by their shoulders to lock into your own eyes, when with a single slight nod, that gaze becomes like a high-speed train that has just run right over everyone else.

He accepted the bid. Two hundred in the back on my left. My heart had been racing for a while now, and I felt the bills in my pockets in bundles dampened by my skin pouring with sweat, by the stifling heat of that room with its garnet red walls glowing like an oven warming the buyers, and by the realization that I couldn't blow this: two hundred once— then I clutched my hands together and hoped no one else would bid, that the fat man in the third row and that woman would for once just shut up so we could put an end to this farce.

Two hundred once, two hundred twice, and playing the role of the man poised to bring down the hammer, he had raised his arm in readiness to let it fall, let it hit the block in front of that whole crowd waiting for what sudden development, so how much, how much will the next bid be? Three hundred? Five hundred?

Twice, thrice, sold to the gentleman in the back on my left, this magnificent straw hat, a fine example of the art.

I believe it was at that instant, seeing Édouard's new and benevolent smile, which seemed almost to congratulate me, that I understood what it means to lose.

And with that single thought I returned to the car. Lise was still waiting for me. I placed the panama casually on the backseat and said: It's time to go now; he's waiting for you. There was the sound of the door slamming shut, then silence: Lise was gone.

SIXTEEN

I SAT THERE BEHIND the wheel without starting the car, out in front of the auction house, leaning back on the headrest as if on a sofa. It was so peaceful not to expect anything more, to simply feel failure take its place inside me like a kindred spirit. Ensconced in the driver's seat, I was waiting for them of course, like a taxi driver, waiting for them both to emerge, and perhaps for him to kiss her, anywhere, there, in the street, on the sidewalk, on the steps of the auction house, kiss her in front of me.

They came out, Lise beside Édouard, and taking her hand in a grasp as firm and shut as a handcuff, he took her over to his car, and I could clearly see that he was taking her by force, pulling on her arm to make her come along, and that neither she nor I could do anything but keep quiet when I felt like shouting, be-

cause it was like an abduction right before my eyes—
a kidnapping, I almost thought, it's a kidnapping,
when I saw her sit in the passenger seat of the Jaguar,
saw him closing the door after her, while I sat alone
and infuriated by that thought now unleashing its infernal autonomy like a high-voltage battery thrum-
ming inside me, like static energy, heavy, painful, like
a lame scenario of what to do or not do, to make it
possible, just possible at some point, to erase forever
all traces of our regrets. That is the only word that
sprang to my lips: *regret.*

They drove off. So did I. I did not play any music
on my car radio. I did not even smoke a cigarette, although I did crack open a window to let in a whiff of
fresh air. I checked the glove compartment to make
sure my revolver was still there, as if to make some
sense of all this. I drove like that through the city
with the warm air blowing in my face, the streets and
shop windows streaming away in the rearview mirror
and back window, and the feeling of being at a film
when the car isn't really moving but there's a movie
screen behind it, as if I were turning the steering
wheel on fake corners, in a fake car, in a fake world. A
real drama, I thought, still following them at a good

distance, their forms barely visible in the dark interior of the Jaguar.

I followed them to the house, still that same house, I told myself again and shook my head in despair at imagining them as a normal couple in a normal life, when I could already see them, him on her in the deep twilight. It was like slides projected by force in my brain, and he was happy, in my head he was happy at their conjoined souls, because of the wind outdoors and the trees like voyeurs, because of something that resembled love, the trees all around bending in the sharp wind and leaning over them.

I parked my car at a distance to avoid attracting suspicion. I took the revolver. I would not use it. I would definitely not use it, but I took it. Keeping my head down, I moved past the high stone walls, crouching like a thief, approaching quietly, inspecting the night and those disturbing shadows, yes, like a common thief; but for a long time now I'd packed my pride away at the bottom of a bag, so, like a common thief I climbed over the wall and I huddled there, in the garden, in the shadows. And I saw them, in front of the sea, outlined there like cut-paper silhouettes.

Lise has never said *kiss me.* To anyone. But with a look or a gesture, it was always like an order coming from far away, from way beyond her shining eyes alive with some strange force that obliged others to comply. And as obligations go, I often thought, there are far worse. It's true, worse was in store for him that evening when he kissed her for the first time in the moonlight, its reflection in the water glowing on their faces, he bending over her, slipping one hand behind her back as if to steady her in the giddiness now possessing him, his heart beating wildly the way it does with each first time.

What possible chemistry might have made this my deliverance, this kiss that would come so belatedly, the headlights of the Jaguar gone black behind them as they drew closer to each other like adolescents who don't know what to do with their bodies. And I watched them, beyond jealousy, beyond suffering; but the sight of her in the darkness bathed in the faint light from the sky, the sight of him clinging to you, Lise, the way an insect circles a streetlamp, yes, like an insect. . . .

I can still see him, leaning with both hands on the low stone wall forming a kind of dike against the waves; he looked like an old captain in the merchant marine at the helm of a ship, standing like a statue on the foredeck, with the garden itself as a kind of prow. He seemed to have commanded the moon to hang there quietly in the sky and the birds to be silent, subdued by the swell; and he'd marked everything's place with a white cross, drawn the horizon with his hands, and the dark island whose granite cliffs could still be divined; and he'd summoned the warm salt air of the sea: everything seemed orchestrated by him, for him, and on high, way up high, I felt, the gods had obeyed him.

Now moonlight was falling on the garden and the wind . . . no, in fact there was no wind; that had dropped, too—everything was falling that day. It's all falling to pieces, I thought. It's lasted a long time: the sea, the house, the dust—everything crumbles. This house doesn't mean anything anymore; perhaps this house has never had any meaning—but today it no longer has any, that's for sure, neither the house nor the skittish pines nor the sea nor the rocks all around. If I were to listen to myself, I'd set it on fire and stand out in front watching it burn: trees make good fuel and all those beams in the ceiling—no, I won't set it on fire.

I thought about how many days we spent simply

walking, Lise and I, and looking at the sky, me telling myself then, for myself alone, that on this earth there had never been anything else. I thought back to the cigarettes on the balcony. I thought that sometimes you wouldn't want anything else from the world.

It wasn't completely dark, because of the natural light from the sky or off the sea, and this mirror effect filled the night with a brightness that seemed tempered for the two of them. I was already thinking: one day someone will replace them here, will have the roses pruned and the tall trees cut down, new wallpaper put up and the gates repainted. Even the odor of tobacco will disappear from the folds of the drapes. There will still be the climbing ivy and the high stone walls, and the anger of the trees on truly windy days. There will still be cold air whistling around the chimney, the same color sky filling the windowpanes, still the musty smell, the attic heat. There will be traces, still traces of them, you must realize this.

Still there in the shadows, I finally went over to the Jaguar. I opened the car door quietly and slid behind the wheel. I almost drove off in it—surely that's what I should have done, it's what anyone else would have done in my place, but me, no, I stayed sitting there and turned on the CD player. The Shostakovich was there and I slipped it in. Go to it, Édouard, kiss her again. Do it, I said, possessed by that single question filling my mind; but it wasn't a question, more like an idea, that everything would soon be over, that soon life would really change; yes, this was like a compulsory refrain that inhabited my night, leaving me sleepless: I could hear myself saying it like you, Lise, that soon life would change.

But how I would have loved to be able to read lips, how I would have loved to hear you, Lise, through the car windows, through the supposed sounds of the sea foam on the rocks, and to know, to know every word exchanged, when even today I can't begin to imagine what you could have told him, with each leaden minute I felt passing, with each word vaguely formed on the curve of your lips. So was I dreaming when I thought I read on those same lips, as if in mute letters, the words *beyond suspicion*? But that's not possible, Lise, that wouldn't have made any sense, would it? I laughed all alone at my doubts. I laughed at having thought that you'd smiled at him. You didn't smile at him, did you?

I thought: no, it's for our own good, all this, for our own good. I thought that once, I thought that twice, but the third time I felt the tears well up. I wondered if the Shostakovich was to blame, that same exhausted waltz, but when I heard the sorrow in it, when I understood what was in your face, now superimposed on the windshield, I collapsed. What impulse of hatred drove me to turn the volume up to the limit? Remote controls on the steering wheel: absolute luxury, I thought. I believe I hummed along with the waltz. And still I saw you, Lise, in the blue night, I saw you but in my head nothing was left. The worn-out waltz, perhaps. The word *dollar.* The word *night.* The word *sister.* Perhaps.

French Fiction from The New Press

THE ABSOLUTE PERFECTION OF CRIME
Tanguy Viel
Translated by Linda Coverdale

The Absolute Perfection of Crime is a novel with all the originality, toughness, and surprises of the best black-and-white film noir. Setting: a small French seaside town. Characters: a group of old crooks, on the verge of retirement. Plot: one final coup—an imaginative and brazen hold-up of the local casino. Thus starts the perfect crime.

978-1-56584-757-6 (hc)

THE LAST FRIEND
Tahar Ben Jelloun
Translated by Linda Coverdale

The Last Friend is a *Rashomon*-like tale of friendship and betrayal set in twentieth-century Tangier. Written in Ben Jelloun's inimitable and powerfully direct style, the novel explores the twists and turns of an intense thirty-year friendship between two young men struggling to find their identities and sexual fulfillment in Morocco in the late 1950s, a complex and contradictory society both modern and archaic.

978-1-59558-008-5 (hc)

MAKING LOVE
Jean-Philippe Toussaint
Translated by Linda Coverdale

Making Love is an original and daring retelling of a classic theme: the end of an affair. Following a couple's final days together in Japan, the novel explores the frustration of two lovers trying to break up with each other while on vacation, even as they go on a wild and intimate ramble through the streets of Tokyo.

978-1-56584-853-5 (hc)

PIANO
Jean Echenoz
Translated by Mark Polizzotti

Max Delmarc, age fifty, is a famous concert pianist with two problems: the first is a paralyzing stage fright for which the second, alcohol, is the only treatment. In this unparalleled comedy from the Prix Goncourt–winning French novelist Jean Echenoz, we journey with Max, from the trials of his everyday life, through his untimely death, and on into the afterlife.

978-1-56584-871-9 (hc)

PIG TALES
Marie Darrieussecq
Translated by Linda Coverdale

Pig Tales is the story of a young woman who slowly metamorphoses into . . . a pig. What happens to her next overturns all our ideas about relationships between man, woman, and beast in a stunning fable of political and sexual corruption.

978-1-56584-442-1 (pb)
978-1-56584-361-6 (hc)

RAVEL
Jean Echenoz
Translated by Linda Coverdale

Ravel is a beguiling and original evocation of the last ten years in the life of a musical genius, written by the acclaimed novelist Jean Echenoz, winner of the Prix Goncourt. Opening in 1927 as Maurice Ravel—dandy, eccentric, and curmudgeon—voyages across the Atlantic aboard the luxurious ocean liner the *France* to begin his triumphant grand tour across the United States, the novel is a truly touching farewell to a dignified and lonely old man going reluctantly into the night.

978-1-59558-115-0 (hc)

SHADOWS OF A CHILDHOOD
Elisabeth Gille
Translated by Linda Coverdale

Before she was killed by the Nazis during World War II, Irène Némirovsky, author of *Suite Française*, sent her two young daughters into hiding, enabling them to survive. The younger daughter, Elisabeth Gille, chronicled her wartime experiences in her own novel, *Shadows of a Childhood*. Gille's haunting book is a moving sequel to her mother's masterpiece and an important part of an extraordinary family's literary legacy.

978-1-59558-356-7 (pb)

THIS BLINDING ABSENCE OF LIGHT
Tahar Ben Jelloun
Translated by Linda Coverdale

Based on an incident involving starvation and torture in Morocco, Prix Goncourt–winner Ben Jelloun's novel is a disturbing, grisly account of how a prisoner survived a twenty-year internment in which he was locked away in a desert tomb.

978-1-56584-723-1 (hc)

THE TROLLEY
Claude Simon
Translated by Richard Howard

From the perch of a wheeled hospital bed, our narrator recalls the trolley that took him to and from school every morning of his childhood—passing back and forth between vine-covered hills, the shore, and the gradually modernizing town. When the past and present collide, the story becomes a fugue of memory that has delighted critics and made the book an immediate bestseller in France.

978-1-56584-857-3 (pb)
978-1-56584-734-7 (hc)

French Nonfiction from The New Press

FRANCE UNDER THE GERMANS
Phillipe Burrin
Translated by Janet Lloyd

France Under the Germans is the definitive study of the choices made by ordinary French citizens during World War II, exposing for the first time the degree of their complicity with the Nazis.

978-1-56584-439-1 (pb)

THE WAR: A Memoir
Marguerite Duras
Translated by Linda Coverdale

Duras's riveting account of life in Paris during the Nazi occupation and the first months of liberation depicts the harrowing realities of World War II–era France. Duras tells of nursing her starving husband back to health after his return from Bergen-Belsen, interrogating a suspected collaborator, and playing a game of cat and mouse with a Gestapo officer who was attracted to her. The result is "more than one woman's diary . . . [it is] a haunting portrait of a time and a place and also a state of mind" (*The New York Times*).

978-1-56584-221-2 (pb)

WARTIME WRITINGS: 1943–1949
Marguerite Duras
Translated by Linda Coverdale

For decades it has been known that Marguerite Duras had kept four notebooks in a blue closet in her country home in France. But until now no one understood the importance of the material that she had written in the period between 1943 and 1949. Here are the first drafts of her most famous works, the true stories behind *The Lover*, *The War*, and several other classics. This book is truly the seventh veil to be lifted by Duras in her multivolume autobiography.

978-1-59558-200-3 (hc)